CUSTOM KILL!

Somehow they had spotted him and circled in behind him. . . .

He dropped to one knee and drew a bead with the big .70-caliber rifle, while calculating the windage and reaching up to adjust the rear sight. McMasters had the lead man beaded, and smiled grimly, knowing what lay in store for him. Gently, he squeezed the trigger, and felt the big rifle butt slam into his shoulder at the same instant he heard the thunderous crack.

He saw the explosion of flesh and bone as the doctored bullet struck home. . . .

McMASTERS

MEXICAN STANDOFF

Lee Morgan

JOVE BOOKS, NEW YORK

MEXICAN STANDOFF

A Jove Book / published by arrangement with
the author

PRINTING HISTORY
Jove edition / February 1996

The Putnam Berkley World Wide Web site address is
http://www.berkley.com

ISBN: 0-515-11808-7

A JOVE BOOK®
Jove Books are published by The Berkley Publishing Group,
200 Madison Avenue, New York, New York 10016.
JOVE and the "J" design are trademarks
belonging to Jove Publications, Inc.

PRINTED IN THE UNITED STATES OF AMERICA

10 9 8 7 6 5 4 3 2 1

One

It was impossibly hot, despite the late hour. Even the breeze, what little there was of it, emphasized the terrible heat. Every time it blew, which was seldom, the tinder-dry grass rattled, and sand sifted across the ground in abrasive clouds. Boyd McMasters could feel the scrape of the sand on the backs of his bronzed hands. When he rubbed his fingers against the three-day growth on his cheeks and chin, sand cascaded into his lap, hissing like snow on a cold winter night, and that sound was the only thing that made the heat bearable. He'd been in blizzards that could freeze a man hard, turn him as white and solid as Lot's wife, and leave him there like a statue, icicles on his eyebrows and chin, for the spring thaw. And he'd been in sandstorms that would peel a man's hide like a skinning knife, right down to raw meat. So when the sand hissed its way into his lap, he thought of the bone-chilling cold of one of those High Plains blizzards, and shivered a little. That must be what they mean by cold comfort, he thought.

But he didn't mind the blizzards and the sandstorms. Not really. He hated the heat, though, and there were times when he wished he could head north, maybe to Colorado or Wyoming, spend the rest of his days, however few or many they might be, catching trout in the Rockies, lay up like a bear over the long, snowbound winters, and lie on his back in a meadow full of paintbrush and columbine once the summer came. But that was just wishful thinking. It was the way a man with time on his hands filled his empty hours, drowning out the tick of the clock, the glue he used to hold those isolated pieces of living together. And Boyd McMasters was a past master of the art.

To look at him, you wouldn't think he was on the short side of thirty. There was something ancient, maybe even timeless, about him. His sandy hair didn't have any streaks of gray in it, but to look at him you had the feeling that that wouldn't last long. The brown eyes, restless and clear, were those of a young man, but they too had something ancient in them, as if he had seen things no man of his years ought to have seen, and as if those things were never very far from his mind, maybe even haunted him a little, prodding him like a bad conscience.

But McMasters didn't have a bad conscience. He was too single-minded for that. He did his job, which he fancied to be part stock detective and part avenging angel, with an implacability that was beyond ruthless and bordered on obsession. That was another way Boyd filled his empty hours, and he had more than his share. His family had been taken from him with an abrupt brutality that had scorched his soul as surely as the raging holocaust that had taken his wife and unborn child had scorched the earth on which his home had stood.

It had been no accident, that fire. It had been deliberately set by the Winslow clan, and Hannah, his expectant wife, had been left, just as deliberately, to burn to death. And Boyd had been forced to stand there helplessly, Hannah's horrible screams ringing in his ears. He had tried to block out the sound, and had wished more than once since that he had gone deaf rather than endure that awful agony. The loss had nearly killed him. The terrible revenge he took on the murderers had come closer to killing him, but when it was all over and every last drop of Winslow blood had seeped into the thirsty sand of the Davis Mountains, he had still been standing, though reduced to a hollow shell, the terrible emptiness yawning inside him unfilled even by the slaughter he had wrought.

It had been a year and a half, but it might just as well have been that morning. Everything was still fresh in his memory, more vivid by far than memories ought to be. He could smell the smoke, feel its heat on his skin, hear the crackle of the burning timbers, taste the ash floating on the wind, and see the transparent orange and blue of the flames as they consumed everything he'd ever cared about. Every sense was drenched in agonizing remembrance, every fiber of his being dyed as black as the charred timbers with the recollection. He had thought then, and sometimes still did, that he would not live long, as if the mysterious force that made the difference between life and death would drain out of him one night in his sleep, leaving behind a parchment bag of brittle bones already half buried in drifting sand. If there was a God, he'd tell himself, that was exactly how it would be.

He had black moods and blacker fits that tempted him to the bottle, where he thought he could hide like a genie, protected from the world by green glass and a piece of cork until some poor unsuspecting fool might find him and unintentionally turn him loose. But as the last year had taught him, things seldom turn out the way a man wished them to, and Boyd McMasters was only the latest man to make that painful discovery.

McMasters looked up at the sky, as he had done countless

times each night, rain or shine, since Hannah's death, and wondered if she was watching over him somehow. He wasn't a religious man, not by a long shot, but he wanted, maybe even had, to believe that she was up there somewhere. If there was an afterlife, she sure as hell would be there. He knew that. And she would be his guardian angel. It was the kind of woman she was, and he needed to know that she hadn't ceased to exist in that horrible conflagration, at least not completely. His world was empty enough as it was, and the idea that Hannah was no longer in it had nearly killed him. Clinging to that one tiny, solitary hope was all that kept him going now.

He'd tried to forget, to drown himself in whiskey, and when that didn't work, in the perfume of a dozen whores, but neither had worked for him. And then he had gone to Oklahoma City, thinking to see his older brother, Warren, one last time, and Warren, as he always did, had taken Boyd by the scruff of the neck and hauled him back from the brink. That seemed like an eternity ago, but it had only been a year ago. Now, resigned to the fact that every week would drag itself along until it seemed like a year, he did the only thing he knew how to do—he enforced the law, not the same way he'd done as sheriff of Reeves County, Texas, but as a troubleshooter for the Cattleman's Protective Association. The pay wasn't great, and the work was hard, but at least it gave him a reason to get up in the morning, which was just about all he demanded of life.

Despite the hazy heat of the day, the night sky was black as coal and crystal clear. He lay back, his head on his saddle, and waited for the the first shooting star. That was Hannah's sign to him that she was nearby, and he couldn't sleep without seeing one. The coals of his cookfire crackled, now and then sending up a little plume of winking sparks. It was the only sound he could hear. San Pedro was still thirty miles away, maybe a little more, and he would not be there until mid-afternoon. He would get an early start and . . . There it was, the brilliant streak that seared itself into his eyes, bright enough to see for a while even after it was long gone.

Reassured one more time, he closed his eyes and tried to sleep. It was never easy, and more often than not these days he found himself wondering whether there might be a bottle in his saddlebags. He didn't lean on the rotgut anymore, but a taste now and then settled his nerves, took the edge off a bad time. Martha Blair had been right about the whiskey, as she seemed to have been right about so many other things.

The mere thought of Martha made McMasters cringe a little. He still felt guilty, as if somehow he had been betraying Hannah, but he knew that was a crock. He hadn't done anything Hannah wouldn't have told him to do if only she could. But he pushed the thought of Martha as far back in his mind as he could, concentrating instead on the job ahead.

The Cattleman's Protective Association had sent him into the Nueces Strip because beeves were disappearing by the hundreds. That was not surprising in itself. Everybody knew the Strip by reputation, if no other way. It was a sinkhole, a place where the dregs of humanity settled out of the mix like coffee grounds to the bottom of a cup. If you had your face on a corkboard in a sheriff's office, or your picture was tacked to every tree for a thousand miles in any direction, in the Strip nobody cared.

Ben Allison, the man he was going to see, was different. One of a handful of men who had tried to tame the Strip, carve a legitimate living out of the heart of bandit heaven, he ran a huge spread down near the Rio Grande. Allison had been a Texas Ranger, one of the men sent into the Strip with McNelly in the old days, to try to clean it up. And with McNelly chewing nails and spitting out nickels, it had worked . . . for a while.

But there was something about the area—some said it was the reputation of the Strip, and some said it was something in the air or the water—but whatever the reason, men with histories they'd rather forget, or secrets they had to hide, still found the region congenial. The proximity of the Mexican border was part of the attraction, of course. Whenever things got too hot, you could walk your horse across the shallow river and take your chances with the *federales,* most of whom couldn't have cared less about the presence of a few gringo desperadoes. They were nothing, stray dogs, flies on a horse's butt.

Allison, though, was having trouble keeping his beeves. He and a handful of like-minded men were trying to reclaim the Strip, make it a decent place to live. It was a hardscrabble living, and the arid climate meant you had to have almost limitless spreads where the cattle could run free and forage for their own food. You couldn't watch them closely, because they were spread too widely. All you could do was hope that the weather didn't take more than its fair share, that your neighbors were, if not honest, at least not too greedy, and that when the roundup came, you had more stock than you'd had the year before. Lately, though, things hadn't worked that way. Neighbors were now cussing each other behind each other's backs, wondering who'd taken what from whom. More than once men had come to blows, and Allison knew it wouldn't be long before men would resort to guns instead of fists, provided they weren't run into the poorhouse first.

San Pedro had a reputation every bit as vile as the Strip itself. There weren't too many towns in the stretch of land between the Nueces and Rio Grande Rivers, and that meant men like Allison were cheek by jowl with men like Rip Winslow and his sons, scum who preyed on those around them, using brute force to take what others had earned by bent backs and sweaty brows. And it was now up to Boyd McMasters to find out exactly where those cattle were disappearing to, and who was pocketing the money.

McMasters slept fitfully, his restless mind churning, his nerves humming like telegraph wires. He never really sank into a deep sleep, but he rested some, and when the sky started to turn gray, he felt he'd gotten all the sleep he was likely to get.

Fixing breakfast over the fire, the new tinder crackling until it vanished under a couple of scrub oak limbs, he watched the sun come up. He had a long ride, and the heat would be blistering, so he was anxious to to get on the trail as soon as possible. His horse seemed to sense his anxiety, pawing the ground and working against the hobble a little to get at a little more nubby grass just out of reach.

He'd camped under a small stand of cottonwoods, beside a tiny creek that couldn't have been a foot deep and barely three times that in width. But the water was fresh, if too warm, and when he'd scrubbed down and dressed, he turned the big roan loose to let it drink a bit and eat a little of the tall grass at the water's edge. Scattering the coals and kicking dirt over them, he poured out the last of his coffee, rinsed the pot in the creek, and packed his gear. He might not have been ready, but it was time, and he saddled the roan, swung up, and headed southeast, toward San Pedro, at a fast trot.

McMasters wanted to get as far as he could before the sun got too high in the sky. There wasn't much relief from the brutal heat, and unless he made better time than he figured to, more than likely he'd have to lay over at the next watering hole just to get out of the sun.

He'd ridden no more than fifteen miles when he spotted a thick plume of dust heading due south, about five or six miles away. It was so dark that at first he'd thought it was smoke, but when he turned field glasses on it, he could see the difference. Whatever kicked it up was pretty sizable, probably several hundred animals. Wild horse herds were scarce in this part of Texas, and that many men on horseback would constitute a small army—which wasn't very likely. That left cattle, a pretty good-sized herd, and the question was whether or not it was legitimate. He was still too far from San Pedro for it to be Ben Allison's stock, unless it had been stolen, but he decided to change course and have a look.

As usual, he was packing a pair of Colt .44's. But they weren't six-shooters. McMasters had learned the art of gunsmithing, and he'd stripped down and rebuilt the Colts, redesigning the cylinders to hold seven rounds instead of the usual half dozen. It had taken some doing, and more geometry than Boyd had cared for, but it worked, and it had already saved his life more than once. Most outlaws didn't know much, but they all could count.

One of the pistols was fully loaded, but the other had two empty shells in the cylinder, and he popped them out and reloaded with a pair of his custom-made rounds. The brass of the tacks inserted into the slugs glinted brightly against the dull gray of the lead. Holstering the pistols again, he loosened his rifle in its boot, just in case. Like the Colts, the rifle was something special. Its octagonal barrel often caused it to be mistaken for a Sharps buffalo gun, but this was not an adaption, it was a Boyd McMasters original, .70-caliber, its rounds tacked like those of the pistols and even more deadly. On impact, the tacks fragmented the softer lead, and had almost explosive results. The rifle could knock down a wall, but it was not just about firepower. The gun was accurate enough, as Boyd liked to say, to knock a tick off a deer at half a mile.

He could feel the hair standing up on the back of his neck, a feeling he'd come to trust. At the bottom of that thick, brown cloud lay trouble. Kicking the big roan into a gallop, he angled toward the swirling cloud of dust. Close as it was, San Pedro would just have to wait a few more hours.

Two

Closing on the cloud of dust, McMasters slowed a little, not wanting to signal his presence by kicking up a dust trail of his own. The herd, and he could see now that that was what it was, was making good time. Nearly a dozen drovers were pushing the animals at a fast clip, obviously in a hurry to get somewhere. That the herd was headed south was odd, but not proof that they had been rustled. Some Mexican rancheros bought beeves north of the border. The Texan stock was hardy, and despite their animosity toward the Mexicans, the ranchers in the Strip had to sell their stock when and where they could.

The cowboys Boyd saw were a mix. Some were dressed like Mexican *vaqueros*, replete with broad-brimmed hats, even a couple of sombreros, and using Spanish saddles, while the rest were scruffy Texans, their shirts less colorful, the sleeves snugger than the puffy cut fancied by the more stylish Mexicans. The terrain was nearly flat, rolling hills barely higher than a man's head, and as the Rio Grande drew nearer, it would flatten still more, making it difficult for McMasters to get very close without being seen. But he thought it might be worth a try.

Sitting on a low rise, the field glasses draped on his chest by their worn leather strap, he watched for several minutes, debating whether to turn off and head for San Pedro or tag along a while yet, see what might catch his eye. He considered even riding right up to the drovers, asking for directions. That might let him get a close-up look, maybe tell him something useful, grist for the mill. He decided on the latter option.

Pushing the roan into a fast trot, he covered the last mile and a half in a few minutes, not worrying now about being seen. In fact, it was to his advantage to call attention to himself, in order to dispel any suspicions about his presence. He was only three hundred yards from the drag rider now, whose job was to eat a lot of dust and keep the stragglers in line, when two men peeled off from the rear of the herd and turned their mounts toward him.

McMasters took off his Stetson and waved it overhead, but the two men approaching him did not respond. One of them leaned over to say something to his companion, but they were too far away for McMasters to hear what was said.

The man in the lead, a thickset Texan whose shirt was stretched taut over a considerable paunch, pulled his pistol at a hundred yards, and it was all McMasters could do to keep himself calm, not drawing one of the Colts and plugging the unfriendly cuss.

At fifty yards, the lead man shouted, "The hell you want, cowboy?"

Taking a deep breath, McMasters lied. "I think I'm lost."

"You following us?" the man asked, only twenty-five yards away now, his gun in his lap, the barrel resting on the saddle horn.

"Sort of. I saw your dust, figured maybe you could give me some directions."

The thick man seemed to relax a little, but he kept his gun

handy, reining in and turning to his companion. The second man was much smaller, but had the same general shape, like a scale model of the first. Reaching up with his left hand, the reins still curled in his fist, the bigger man brushed his knuckles against a thick, black mustache coated with the thick beige dust. "Where you headed?"

"San Pedro."

"You're way off line, cowboy," the man said. "You want to head due east. You got business there?"

McMasters shook his head. "Nope. Heard there might be some jobs, and I could use one."

"No jobs in San Pedro, partner. I can tell you that. You want rotgut whiskey, or worn-out whores, you got a chance, but work you ain't gonna find none. Believe me. What kind of job you lookin' for?"

"Just about anything that pays a fair wage'd be all right with me."

"Fair wage or slave wage, it don't make no difference. There's precious little work to be had, and more than a few trail bums sleepin' in the streets already waitin' for what little work there is."

"Too close to turn back now, I reckon."

"Might be so. But if you got a few dollars in your jeans, you'd be best off heading north, up around Austin."

"How about your outfit? You need a good hand?"

The portly man shook his head. He looked annoyed now, and he was tensing up again. "I just told you, cowboy. Ain't no work to be had."

"What outfit you with?"

The man sucked a tooth, wiggling his mustache in the process, before answering. "Triple Bar. Bartholomew Kelly's outfit. Ever heard of it?"

McMasters shook his head. "Can't say as I have. But then,

I don't know much about Texas. Wouldn't have got myself lost if I did, I guess.''

The littler man was getting impatient, and nudged his horse out from behind his larger companion. He wore a flowery Mexican shirt with ruffled sleeves, and a leather sombrero that made him look like some sort of colorful mushroom. "Gringo, you heard the man, he tole you there ain't no jobs. Now why don't you turn your gringo ass around and go back where you come from?"

"Hold on there, Carlito," the bigger man said. "No call to be so surly with the man. He's just lost, is all. Neighborly thing to do is point him in the right direction."

But Carlito was not about to be mollified. "You already pointed. But he don't want to listen."

McMasters raised his hands a little, trying to calm the peppery *vaquero* down a little. "Too much jalapeno in your eggs this morning, amigo?" he asked, giving the man his best smile.

The Mexican reached for his pistol, but the big man caught his wrist and forced the revolver back into its holster. He turned to look at McMasters, still keeping his hand on the Mexican's wrist. "Look, mister, maybe you best ride on. We got work to do and its too damn hot to be arguing with anybody."

"Fair enough," McMasters said. "Much obliged for the directions." He glanced at the herd. "Good-lookin' beeves," he said. "Must be five, six hundred head. Where you headed with them? Mexico?"

"Maybe you should mind your own business, amigo," Carlito said.

McMasters grinned, nodding agreeably. "Maybe," he said. He waved, then spurred the roan and headed east. It was afternoon, and the sun behind his back spilled a long shadow well out ahead of him. Something about the encounter bothered him. Carlito for sure, but then he was used to surly cowboys, and Mexicans were no different. The work was hard, the hours were long, and the pay was fitful and never enough, not with the thirst you acquired eating a couple cubic yards of dirt everyday.

He wished he had gotten closer to the herd, close enough to check out the brands and earmarks on the bigger beeves, but that would have been pushing it, and with Carlito so prickly, it could have gotten ugly in a hurry. McMasters was not one to back down from a fight, but he didn't want to do anything that might make his job tougher, because it was tough enough already. If the herd was legitimate, all he would have succeeded in doing was alienating somebody he might have to count on in the near future. If it wasn't, he might have gotten himself killed.

Either way, it wouldn't have done the Cattleman's Protective Association much good. Since they were paying his salary, it behooved him to be mindful of their interests. It was politics, of course, but then McMasters had never seen anything that involved large sums of money that didn't also involve a generous helping of the art of compromise.

He looked back over his shoulder and realized that Carlito was watching him. If he didn't know better, McMasters would have sworn the *vaquero* had actually followed him a hundred yards or so. The cloud of dust kicked up by the herd was receding to the southeast, and he knew the drovers were pushing it straight for the border.

Fifteen minutes later, he turned again, but this time Carlito was nowhere in sight. Must have gone back to the herd, McMasters thought, but he wasn't as sure as he wanted to be. Something about the pugnacious *vaquero* waved a red flag in the back of his mind. It had been obvious that Carlito was looking for trouble, but McMasters couldn't decide whether it was just his personality, or if something more urgent were at the root of his behavior.

If the beeves were stolen, that would go a long way to explain the angry nervousness the two men had demonstrated. But why didn't they just shoot him when they had the chance? But if the beeves weren't stolen, then what was eating Carlito? Questions, McMasters thought, always questions. Why in hell weren't answers as easy to come by?

As near as he could judge, he was still about ten miles from San Pedro, and from what he'd heard, he'd have to look sharp to avoid riding right past it without ever realizing it was there. It was just a ramshackle collection of weathered buildings, most of them one story and longtime strangers to the tickle of a brush full of paint or whitewash.

He pulled out his pocket watch, tilting it to keep the sun from glancing off the crystal and blinding him. Quarter after three. Cottonwood crowns about a mile ahead marked the next water. He was hot, thirsty, and dusty. He could rest for an hour and still make San Pedro well before nightfall.

Changing direction slightly to head for the trees, he watched them take shape in the afternoon shimmer. As the trunks of the tall trees came into view, they wriggled like snakes underwater, sometimes disappearing altogether as the heated air shimmied and swirled. The terrain changed a bit, the hills rolling more, and as he topped a rise, he could look down into a broad valley no more than twenty or twenty-five feet below the crest on which he sat.

A wide creek, lined by clumps of brush and tall grass on both sides, snaked across the valley floor, its margin a few feet of bright green against the yellowed sweep of dry grass. Glints of sunlight flashed in the brush where the water ran rough. McMasters aimed for the trees, dismounting a few yards before reaching them and turning the horse loose to graze while he walked to the bank and knelt on the lush carpet of grass. Taking off his hat, he leaned over and im-

mersed his head, using his hand to splash water on the back
of his neck and rinse off the thick coating of sweaty dust
that felt like library paste to his fingers.

The water was warm, but after the blazing sun, it felt cool
to the touch. Spluttering and shaking his head, he sent arcs
of water in every direction, and a tiny rainbow appeared in
a shaft of brilliant sunlight spearing through the cottonwood
foliage. He rinsed his mouth, spat out the muddy water, and
then drank, a small mouthful at first, then deeply. He felt
better already, the sensation of the water flooding his body
the same way the heat of cheap whiskey used to percolate
from his gut to the tips of his extremities. Another sip, and
he lay back on the grass, his hat resting on his stomach.

He stared up at the waving leaves, then closed his eyes
when the leaves fluttered in the breeze and the sun came
glaring through for a moment. He opened them again when
a shadow fell across his face. He sat up abruptly, then relaxed
when he realized it was just the leaves shifting again.

Something caught his attention out beyond the brush,
maybe a shadow, maybe some movement against the wind.
Whatever it was, he turned, starting to get to his knees. A
twig snapped, and he was on his feet now, moving toward
the brush, his hand already dropping to the butt of his Colt.
Ducking to his left, he moved into some thick undergrowth.
He swept the thorny branches aside, not worrying about the
noise.

The crack of a pistol caught him by surprise. The bullet
whined past him, snipping leaves and snapping a branch just
inches from his left shoulder. He saw the flash, then for an
instant a shadow and a splash of bright color. Immediately,
he thought of Carlito's shirt. Thumbing the hammer back on
his Colt .44, he edged to the left, dropped to one knee, and
waited.

He was stuck. Move into the clear, and he gave the edge

to the hidden gunman. Fire blind, and he gave away his position. All he could do was wait. The clock ticked. One minute, then two and three. Not a sound from the brush. The color hadn't reappeared among the dark green leaves, and he was starting to think he'd been outfoxed. He groped in the grass until he found a small rock, no larger than a strawberry, and tossed it into the shrubbery. He heard it land, clinking on another stone. But there was no response.

He lay on the ground then, snaking under the brush, looking for any telltale sign, maybe sunlight on a spur, the scuffed brown of a well-worn boot, faded denim. But all he saw was green in a dozen shades. He was trying now to be silent, easing his way out into the grass. He heard footsteps then, at some distance, and scrambled out away from the brush, getting to his feet in the same motion. He saw the color again, and started to run as the fleeing gunman vaulted into the saddle of a free-standing horse several hundred yards away.

His own horse and the rifle were on the other side of the brush. As the gunman's horse started to move, McMasters dropped to one knee, braced his right hand with his left, knowing the range was too great, and snapped off a shot, then another. The gunman turned once, his face a beige blur. The shirt was brightly colored, but the sleeves were tight, rolled to the elbow. It wasn't Carlito. Cursing, McMasters holstered the Colt.

But at least, he thought, I put a burr under somebody's saddle.

Three

·

McMasters kept an eye peeled all the way into San Pedro. He was convinced now that the herd he'd seen had been stolen cattle. There was no other credible explanation for the attempted bushwhacking. As far as he knew, no one but Ben Allison knew he was coming, so it must have been a guilty conscience, or fear of discovery, that had prompted the attack. But no harm had been done, and McMasters was used to watching his back. All this meant was that he'd have to be as careful as usual.

San Pedro was everything he'd expected, and less. The edge of town sported a weatherbeaten sign, its ancient paint flaking away like dead skin, the letters and numerals it once bore no longer readable. The buildings themselves were rundown, their boards split and gray, a few strips of old paint curled here and there, fluttering in the hot breeze. The wood reminded him of old bones that had lain in the sun and the rain for several years, like the skeletons of slaughtered buffalo the bone-pickers hadn't yet gotten to.

San Pedro wasn't a cow town exactly, but it was closer to one than to anything else. As he rode down the main street, he counted four saloons, all of them already crowded. The

tinkle of an out-of-tune piano from one on his right clashed
with the boinging plink of a banjo from one directly across
the street. Everything about the place was gray, including the
music. It even seemed that the sun itself was less effective
in the dusty streets, as if something about San Pedro was
soaking it up.

The San Pedro Hotel was the only three-story building,
and it looked rickety enough to scare off the faint of heart.
Its sign hung from three lengths of rusted chain, and
streaks of reddish brown stained the sign's white background. The ground floor featured a restaurant and saloon,
each with its own entrance, and disreputable though the
hotel was, it looked as good a place to stay as any. Dismounting in front of it, he tied up at a splintery hitching
rail, shook the dust from his clothes, and clapped his jeans
with his hat before climbing onto the weathered boardwalk.
He went inside the lobby, his boots sending little puffs of
dust up from the threadbare carpet, and tapped a bell on
the scarred top of the registration desk.

A skinny kid in a blue and white striped shirt, garters
holding the rolled sleeves to the middle of his forearms,
looked up from behind the desk. His hands were inkstained,
and his pointy, rat-like teeth were dyed yellow. He wore
wire-rimmed spectacles that pinched his skinny nose tighter
still, and when he spoke, his voice cracked. "Can I help you,
mister?"

"Like a room for a few days."

"Pay by the day or the week? Week's cheaper."

"The week'll be fine. How much?"

"Three dollars." He eyed McMasters suspiciously, then
added, "In advance."

McMasters fished three coins from his jeans pocket and
stacked them with a musical clink on the scarred wood.
The kid looked at them, then turned the register around

and handed him a pen, a fresh drop of ink running down the length of one finger and plopping audibly on the open book. The kid looked at the ink, then at McMasters, who said, "Maybe you want to wipe that mess up before I sign?"

The kid curled his lip as if the request were impertinent, but grabbed a blotter already stained dark blue, and slid its edge into the drop, watching the dampness spread and darken the paper. A shiny blue disk remained behind, and the kid set the blotter on top of it and pressed with the heel of his hand. "That suit you?" he asked, pulling the blotter away.

"It'll do." McMasters signed his name in a tight, neat hand, then spun the register around and slid it back to the clerk.

The kid adjusted his glasses, leaned a little closer to the ledger, and said, "Boyd McMasters. That you?"

McMasters nodded. "I'll be wantin' a hot bath. I don't suppose you have plumbing, do you?"

"As a matter of fact, we do. The end of the hall. You need a key, though, and it costs fifty cents."

"In advance, I suppose?"

The kid chuckled. "You're a fast learner, Mr. McMasters."

"You don't know the half of it, kid."

"You can have some assistance with your bath, if you like."

"I can handle a washrag and a bar of soap with the best of them."

The kid wiggled his eyebrows, then leered. "That wasn't the kind of assistance I was talking about, know what I mean?"

"You mean a woman, that it?"

The clerk nodded.

"How much?"

"The house gets a dollar. The rest depends on how much

assistance you require. You work that out with the bath attendant."

"Negotiable, is it?"

The kid grinned. "Yes, sir."

"It's been a long ride. I reckon I could use a little assistance."

The kid slapped the desktop, then turned and jerked a key off a metal hook and slid it to McMasters. "Third floor, Room Five, on your left. I'll send the attendant whenever you say."

"No time like the present, I reckon."

McMasters hoisted his saddlebags to his shoulder and jingled the key ring in his right hand as he climbed the stairs. In his left, he felt the weight of his rifle. When he glanced back at the desk, the clerk was leering at him again. The kid waved, then disappeared into a back room. The air in the stairwell was close, viscous as oil, and stank of stale booze and sour perfume. By the time McMasters reached the third floor, he felt as if he couldn't breathe.

The corridor on the top floor was a little better, and he noticed windows open at either end, letting the air circulate a little. He imagined the room would be a sweatbox, but he was bone tired, and as long as it had a bed, he wouldn't complain. He found Room 5, opened the rattling lock, and pushed the door open. The room was sparsely furnished, and had the same overpowering scent of cheap perfume. A bed covered with a thick comforter, a night table by the bed's side, a small kerosene lamp on the table, and a pair of high-backed chairs comprised the complete furniture inventory.

He dropped his saddlebags on the bed, then leaned the rifle against the wall between the headboard and the night table. Turning away from the uprush of perfumed air, he sat down and pulled off his boots. Standing again, he took off his gunbelt, draped it over one of the chair backs, and opened his saddlebags. He had a clean shirt and pair of jeans in one bag, along with shaving gear and a bar of brown lye soap.

He wasn't much taken with the idea of bedding down with a "bath attendant," but he knew that whores were common in San Pedro. Cowhands, honest and crooked alike, dropped their pay on whiskey and women. You couldn't ask a bottle any questions, and that left the women. In his experience, McMasters had found that men liked to talk, telling women who had no hold on them things they would tell no one else. Half of it and more was bullshit, but no matter how great the exaggeration, there was often a kernel of truth somewhere in the middle. If he found the right woman, and asked the right questions, he could save himself a lot of time and trouble.

He wanted to see Ben Allison, but that was best done after a night's sleep. He was tired and he did need a bath, so he might as well kill a pair of birds. As he sat down on the bed again, a knock on the door stopped him. He walked to the door in his stockinged feet and leaned close to the panel. "Who is it?"

"You wanted a bath, *señor*?" The voice was musical, and sounded younger than he'd expected. Most whores were old before their time, and looked and sounded even older than they were. He imagined the same applied to bath attendants at the San Pedro Hotel.

He opened the door and stepped back, surprised at how attractive the young woman in the doorway was. She couldn't have been more than eighteen, and her face was smooth, even a little chubby with the last bit of baby fat. No wrinkles, no crow's-feet, and no scars. Whoever she was, she was new at her trade. As she stepped into the room, McMasters realized that she was rather tall, maybe five seven or thereabouts, and except for the rounded cheeks, she was slender. She smiled at him, clearly nervous, and held out a

thick towel and patted it. There was no hint of perfume about
her, cheap or otherwise, and McMasters thanked his lucky
stars.

"My name is Margarita, *señor*."

McMasters nodded. "You can call me Boyd."

"Pleased to meet you, *Señor* Boyd. My English is not so
good, so if I mistake myself, please don't be angry, all
right?"

McMasters was taken with her immediately. She seemed
so innocent, too innocent to be working in a place like this.
"Well," he sighed, "to tell you the truth, Margarita, there
are times when my English ain't so good either."

"You want a bath, *señor*?" She nodded eagerly, as if trying to coax him into it, and he hemmed and hawed a bit.
Margarita was not what he'd had in mind.

"Actually, I do, Margarita. But what I want even more is
some sleep, and a little companionship."

She looked crestfallen. "Did I offend you, *señor*?"

McMasters hurriedly shook his head. "No, no, not at all.
It's just that I . . . well, to tell you the truth, you seem so
young, and . . ."

"I am good at my job, *Señor* Boyd." She seemed hurt.

"I'm sure you are. But . . ."

She walked to the bed and sat down on it, plumping the
ruffled skirt of her dress and tugging at its low-cut bodice,
trying to exaggerate the curve of exposed flesh. She crossed
her legs, revealing a trim ankle, and leaned backed in what
was an unintentional parody of seduction.

McMasters smiled. She reached behind her back and
jerked her arms toward him, and the bodice came away to
her waist. Full breasts, firm as pomegranates, their nipples
dark and swollen, heaved as she breathed, a trickle of sweat
glistening between them. She cupped her breasts in her hands
and gave him a pouty smile.

McMasters went to her and knelt in front of her. "Margarita, you're beautiful, I can see that. But believe me, all I want right now is some talk."

She was on the verge of tears now, and McMasters tried to console her. "Listen, I'll pay. You don't have to worry about getting into trouble. All right?"

She nodded uncertainly, lay back on the bed, and tugged off her dress. Dressed now only in pair of ruffled knickers, she scooted back along the bed and patted the pillow beside her. "We talk here, *señor*. Then maybe . . ."

McMasters started to respond, but she patted the pillow again, this time more assertively. "Here, *señor*." He walked around the bed and sat on the opposite side, then leaned back.

She turned then, rested her head on his shoulder, and brought his hand to her breast. "What do you want to talk about, *señor*?"

In spite of his determination to resist her abundant charms, he rubbed his thumb on an erect nipple. "Oh, you know, lots of stuff. It's been a long time since I had a good talk. What's it like in San Pedro?"

She shrugged. "Like you would expect. There is a lot of drinking. A lot of cowboys. Men shoot each other and they spend their money on whiskey and women."

She started to rub McMasters's chest, slipping her hand inside his shirt. She was attractive, no doubt about that, and the feeling made him uncomfortable. He kept thinking about Hannah, and about the weeks' worth of grime clinging to his skin. He sat up, and leaned over to kiss her on the forehead.

"I have an idea," he said.

"What?"

"How about if I go on down the hall and take a bath. Then when I come back, we can talk. I'll feel better once I get cleaned up."

"I can come with you," she suggested.

McMasters shook his head. "No, no need, Margarita. You just wait here." He stood up, grabbed the towel, and held out his hand for the key to the bathroom. Chewing on her lower lip, she finally relented, dropped the key into his palm, and lay back on the bed, once more trying her damnedest to look seductive, but succeeding only in reminding him just how young she was.

He knew that a lot of men would have jumped at the chance to bed her, and only dimly understood his own reluctance. It had to do with Hannah, and to a lesser extent with Martha Blair. He knew himself well enough to know that. But that only explained part of his hesitation. Maybe, he thought, I can figure out while I soak off the trail dust.

Four

Refreshed from a good night's sleep, the first in a week, McMasters rose early. He felt nearly civilized as he dressed, and when he went down to the restaurant for breakfast he was in a good mood, or as close to one as he came these days. His waitress was Margarita, and she smiled pleasantly as he ordered steak and eggs and a cup of coffee. There was no hint of collusion, no nervous darting of her eyes. She was going to watch, and keep her ears open, or so she'd said. And McMasters hoped she was as good as her word.

The food came quickly, and he wolfed it down. He left Margarita a hefty tip and headed for the livery stable, the .70-caliber rifle under his arm. He was actually looking forward to meeting Ben Allison. Old-time Texas Rangers were a breed apart, their reputations so embellished over the years that, to most people, they were somewhere between men and gods. Rip Ford, McNelly, Lee Hall—these were the Texas version of Ajax and Achilles, men who looked death in the face, gave the tobacco an extra chew or two to work up a good dose of juice, then spat right in its eye. And Ben Allison was among their company.

The Rocking A, Allison's spread, was five miles southeast

of San Pedro. According to Margarita, the Brownsville Road led right past the front gate. He couldn't miss it, she'd told him.

It was another scorcher of a day, but it was still early, and the heat was bearable if not pleasant. Two miles from town, he encountered a surrey with an attractive woman at the reins. Judging by her jet-black hair and the slightly Indian cast of her features, she was probably Mexican. He touched the brim of his hat, but the woman ignored him, snapping the reins a couple of times as if to widen the gap between them more quickly.

Twenty minutes later, he found the main gate, a tall arch painted white, a foot-high replica of the Rocking A brand affixed to its center. The gate was open, and McMasters rode through, staring down the long approach at a rambling Mexican-style hacienda. Flowers lined both sides of the lane, and semi-circular beds of neatly tended petunias, marigolds, and geraniums fronted the low stone walls that surrounded the house. The earth around the flowers was dark, and beads of water shook like diamonds on the dark green leaves of the plants. Someone had been gardening already, despite the early hour.

McMasters tied off at a hitching post and looked up at the terra-cotta roof tiles arranged neatly like the scales of a fish. The only relief in the shiny brown expanse was another replica of the Rocking A, laid in white tiles dead center on the sloping roof. Those tiles would have cost a pretty penny, McMasters thought.

Inside the walls, gravel beds studded with cacti and yucca sported several birdbaths that looked like some sort of ceramic mushrooms. Stepping onto the flags of the veranda, McMasters felt a little nervous. He hadn't expected such grandeur in so godforsaken a place as the Nueces Strip. Ben Allison, whatever his current troubles might prove to be, had done all right for himself. That much was clear.

McMasters was about to knock on the jamb of the open doors, but someone inside the house had spotted him. "Looking for somebody, cowboy?"

"Ben Allison," McMasters answered, leaning into the dim light of the interior but still unable to see anyone. "He around?"

"Who wants to know?"

"I do. Name's McMasters, Boyd McMasters."

"Warren's little brother?" The question was followed through the door by the imposing figure of a silver-maned mountain of a man, approaching with his hand outstretched. "Come on in, Mr. McMasters. I'm Ben Allison."

Allison stood in the doorway now, his head bent a little to clear the low lintel. The dark bronze of his skin was creased with wrinkles, but that and the white hair were the only suggestions of age about him. Unlike most men who had attained considerable success, his stomach gave no evidence of it. It was taut and probably rock hard. McMasters took the offered hand, and the grip was firm and sure as Allison squeezed and shook. "Pleased to meet you, Boyd. I had a letter from Warren a week or so back. Said he was sending somebody down, but didn't say who. I reckon I should count myself lucky. Got me the top dog, from what I hear."

Hardened though he was, McMasters was pleased. The idea of a legend like Ben Allison being impressed by his credentials was enough to give him a swelled head, but he knew that being accorded respect by the rancher was one thing. Keeping it was another.

"You probably passed Carmen on the way into town," Allison said.

"Carmen?"

"My wife. Second wife actually. I lost Martha more than

twenty years back. Carmen took the surrey into San Pedro
to pick up a few things. You'll stay with us, won't you?''

McMasters shook his head. "Actually, I thought it would
better if I stayed in town. That way, I might be able to pick
up some useful information. And the fewer people who know
who I am and why I'm here, the better."

"Maybe so, but San Pedro ain't no bed of roses. You got
a couple of rooming houses that ain't nothin' but whorehouses and that fleabag hotel to choose from. Slim pickin's,
you ask me."

"You'd be surprised what you can learn in a place like
that, if you keep your ear to the ground."

"Well," Allison said, "have it your way. But we can talk
about that later. Come on inside. I'll fill you in on what's
been goin' on around here." The big rancher turned and
waited for McMasters to precede him into the house. Clapping one thick hand on Boyd's shoulder, Allison ushered him
down a hall, its wooden floors gleaming with a recent coat
of shellac, and led him into a high-ceilinged room that must
have been his study. Two walls were book-lined, the gold
stamping on the spines of the leather-bound volumes gleaming softly in the sunlight filtering through a gauzy curtain.

"Some place you have here, Mr. Allison."

"Call me Ben, Boyd. And yeah, it's somethin', all right.
I thank you kindly for the compliment. I built it for Carmen
a few years back. She's Mexican, and she comes from a
wealthy family. I figured I owed it to her to build her a place
like she was used to. Tough enough putting up with an old
buzzard like me, without having to come down in the world
too."

Allison walked behind a large walnut desk and lowered
himself gracefully into a high-backed leather armchair. In-
dicating a similar chair on the opposite side of the desk, he
said, "Make yourself comfortable."

As McMasters sat down, Allison bent over. The rumble of a drawer being opened was followed by the clink of glassware, and the rancher hauled out a decanter of whiskey and a pair of shot glasses. He poured two stiff ones, shoved one across the gleaming desktop with his fingertips, and picked up the other in a massive fist. "Bourbon, straight from the mother lode," he said, flashing a broad grin. Then he downed the drink in a single swallow.

Boyd sipped his, then set it on the desk still half full. "Why don't you tell me about the troubles you've been having. Warren gave me a broad sketch before I left, but I'd like to hear it from you, if you don't mind."

"Not at all. Before I do, though, let me tell you that it galls me some to even have to get in touch with the Association. You got to understand that I am a man used to taking care of his own business. But things are getting way out of hand down this way, and I am not as young as I used to be. Not by a long shot."

"Understood."

"Well, sir, then I guess I might as well start at the beginning. You know a little about the Strip, I suppose. You can't hardly be in your line of work without having heard something. Used to be, when I first come this way with Captain McNelly, you couldn't throw a rock into a crowd without hitting a wanted man. Every cutthroat and roughneck from New York to California seemed to know how to get here, and once he did, he made hisself to home. Den of thieves, and all that. Course, if you're gonna make a living on that side of the law, then pretty soon you got to start looking elsewhere for your money. Don't do no good to keep robbin' from each other and passin' the same few dollars from hand to hand. Once they realized that, the scum that made the Strip a living hell started to use it as kind of a hidey-hole. They'd go off for a month or two at a time, steal

what they could, and come on back to lay low for a while.
There wasn't no law to speak of down here, and lawmen
from other parts weren't too anxious to pay a visit.''

"That why the Rangers were sent in?"

"That was one reason. The other was that U.S. marshals'd
get sent in and just plain disappear. Never be heard from
again. Like they walked right off the edge of the earth, or
something. They'd find a body now and then, of course, but
long past tellin' who it was. You could tell he was a lawman
by the rusted star layin' there in the bones, but that was about
all.''

"When was this?"

"It started right after the Civil War, '66 or '67, I guess.
You got to realize, once the war was over, there was a lot
of men who didn't know how to farm or work for their daily
bread. They didn't have two pennies to rub together neither.
All they knew was ridin' and killin'. And the South was
fallin' to pieces. There weren't no jobs because the factories,
such as they were, had been destroyed. Not like up North. It
was hardscrabble farmin' mostly, and with money hard to
come by, there wasn't much chance of anybody scrapin'
enough together to buy land if he didn't already own it. Fact
is, lots of folks lost everything they had. You put a lot of
angry men with blood in their eyes into a situation like that,
you get a recipe for trouble sure as I'm sittin' here. Word
got around that the Strip was the place to go if you had
somethin' to hide, or a skeleton in your closet. So the governor sent McNelly's Rangers in to clean up the Strip, gave
Captain McNelly this big old book with lists of wanted men
from all over creation. If the captain got his hands on you,
God help you if your name was in that book. The end of a
short rope was all you had to look forward to more often
than not.''

"Sounds kind of like what happened in Oklahoma before

they opened the Indian Territory up for settlement by whites.''

"It was. It was exactly like that. Hell, half the men old Isaac Parker hung were run down in the Indian Nation. Weren't no law there neither. And believe you me, they didn't call him the Hanging Judge for no reason. Anyhow, after McNelly was done, the Strip was livable. Not tame exactly, but passable. And the governor realized that to keep it that way, he had to encourage law-abiding folks to settle here, let them outnumber the remnants of the outlaw bands, give them something to defend, a reason to fight for law and order. That's when I started the Rocking A. I was getting a little long in the tooth for three-day rides and sleeping in the rain, so I decided I'd settle down. Best thing I ever did. It was rough in the early days, make no mistake, but we got over the bumps after a time. Until recently, that is.''

"As I understand it from Warren, you and some of the other big ranchers have been losing quite a lot of livestock.''

"Losing? Huh, that ain't the half of it. Hemmorhaging is more like it. I lost more than two thousand beeves the last three months. Some other ranchers have lost even more than that. There ain't but a dozen big spreads in the whole Strip, but every last one of them has lost a bunch of cattle.''

"What about the smaller outfits? They lose anything?''

"Some, but not much. Oh, I know what you're thinkin'. You're thinkin' maybe it's the little guys, trying to get fat off ranchers like me. But we considered that, looked into it. And it don't seem likely. It takes a lot of men to push a big herd around in a hurry. Hell, I got near forty men workin' for me, and it's all they can do to ride herd on my holdings. A little guy can't pay too many men, and he can't spare the ones he's got for no midnight rides. If they're running off my stock, they're getting rid of it right quick. They ain't taking it home and doctoring the brands. And it ain't so much calves we're losing as full-grown, market-ready beeves. Money in the bank, they are, *if* you got a place to unload them.''

"Mexico?"

"Most likely. There or Brownsville. There's a lot of shipping out of Brownsville, and out of Matamoras, just across the border, on the Gulf like Brownsville. It ain't but three or four more miles, and it's a whole lot safer. We sent a man in on our own 'bout six weeks ago. And we ain't seen hide nor hair of him since.''

"Where'd you send him?"

"Brownsville first. Told him to stay out of Mexico unless he was sure. Them Mexican *federales* are cheaper than two-bit whores. You can buy them with a song and an easy grin, you want to know the truth of it. Course, they ain't paid much by the Mexican government, and half the goddamn officer corps is on the take one way or another. The men go along or they go on home. Watching some major get fat on bribes beats hoeing corn any day of the week, so most of them go along.''

"What about talking to Washington? You tried that?"

"Nope, and we ain't about to. You go through them politicians up North, you got to live long as Methuselah you want to see any results. I ain't got the time nor the inclination.''

"But you don't have any real suspects, is that right?"

Allison poured himself another drink before answering. McMasters picked up his own glass and took another small sip of the bourbon.

Allison grinned. "Smooth as French silk, ain't it?"

McMasters nodded. "I guess. Can't say as I ever seen any French silk.''

"Take my word for it, it's smooth, and this here bourbon is smoother still.''

"I ran into a herd on the way here," McMasters said. "Surly bunch of riders, some Mexican, most Texan."

"What outfit?"

"Triple Bar, they said. Man named Bartholomew Kelly owns it."

"Never heard of the place. Or the man."

McMasters leaned forward. "You sure about that?"

"Damn right," Allison snapped. The old Ranger in him was riled by the challenge, and he didn't mind if McMasters knew it. "I know every damn rancher for a couple hundred miles in any direction, both sides of the border, and I'm tellin' you there ain't no such man. And I know the brand registry for the whole damn state. There ain't no Triple Bar. Not in Texas."

McMasters nodded. "So," he said.

"Yeah. You run smack into 'em, and didn't even know it."

"I won't make that mistake again. And you can take that to the bank."

"You don't get a rope on these bastards right quick, it's the only thing I'll have to take to the bank."

Five

Allison downed another drink. "What do you figure to do first?"

McMasters laughed. "Hell, there are so many loose ends. The only thing to do is start tugging, see what comes apart. For starters, I want to take a closer look at that herd I passed yesterday."

"They're long gone, more than likely. Especially if they were stolen beeves."

"Probably, but I'd still like to see where they went. Maybe that'll give me some idea of what to look for."

"I wouldn't do that by myself, I was you. You better let me send somebody along, just in case."

"I'm not sure that—"

"Look, Boyd. I know your reputation. But I also know this country. You go poking an anthill with a stick around here, what comes out could eat you alive. You let me send somebody with you. I know you want to lay low, and I agree with that. But I'd feel a whole let better knowing you had company. Besides, you'll probably have to cross the border, and the man I have in mind is comfortable on either side of the river."

Without waiting for an answer, he bellowed at the top of his lungs, "Rosalita, you out there?"

He tapped his hand on the desk impatiently, waiting for a reply. After thirty seconds, a beautiful young woman, in all but age a copy of the woman McMasters had passed on the way out from town, stuck her through the doorway. "You called me, Papa?"

Allison lit up. "This is my daughter, Rosalita, Boyd," he said.

McMasters got to his feet as the girl entered the room, bowed graciously, then took her hand. "Boyd McMasters," he said.

"Pleased to meet you, Mr. McMasters," she answered. Her smile was radiant, revealing small, even teeth, white as new ivory. Her black eyes held a mischievous twinkle as they danced from McMasters to her father and back. Although dressed in blue jeans and a denim work shirt, both faded and snug, she looked voluptuous and almost elegant.

Her voice was pure music, and Boyd felt a slight flush rising up the back of his neck. He hoped Ben Allison didn't notice, but the old Ranger was already back to business. "Uncle Miguel around, honey?"

"I saw him a few minutes ago, why?"

"Run and get him for me, would you? Tell him it's important."

She turned, her long black hair billowing around her shoulders, her legs impossibly long, and the movement sent a breath of honeysuckle to surround McMasters. When she was gone, Allison grinned at him. "The apple of my eye," he said. "Nineteen years old, and already she knows more about this place than anybody, including me."

McMasters, not trusting his voice to work properly, just nodded.

Allison hummed to himself, staring intently at the door as

if his attention could hasten the arrival of Uncle Miguel, whoever the hell he might be. In a couple of minutes, McMasters heard the jingle of spurs and the thud of boot heels on the wooden floor. Then a man who bore a striking resemblance to Rosalita Allison appeared in the doorway.

"Miguel, come on in," Allison bellowed, "and close the damn door."

Once Miguel was inside, the door shut behind him, he looked at McMasters curiously. Allison did the introductions. "This here's my foreman and brother-in-law, Miguel Rosales," he said. And he added, "Mike's my wife's younger brother."

Miguel stared at McMasters, his head canted toward Allison, waiting for some explanation, which was not long in coming. "That's Boyd McMasters, Mike. He's down here from the Cattleman's Protective Association. Gonna help us clear up this rustling business."

Again McMasters stood and offered a hand. Miguel Rosales smiled, shook the hand firmly, and then looked at his brother-in-law.

"Boyd seen a herd southwest of San Pedro yesterday," Allison said. "The drovers told him it was Triple Bar stock, belonged to somebody named Bartholomew Kelly."

Miguel laughed. "Never heard of either one, Ben."

"That's what I told Boyd. Told him there weren't no such brand, and if there was such a man as Bartholomew Kelly, I'd never met him."

"Must have been rustled stock," Miguel said. Looking at McMasters, he added. "Sounds like you got a close-up look at the problem already."

McMasters shrugged. "I guess."

"Boyd wants to track the herd a ways, even cross the border if he has to, and I told him it'd be best if he had somebody along, ride shotgun so to speak. Especially once he got into Tamaulipas. I figured you're the best man for the job. He runs into any trouble, having a relative of the provincial governor along would be mighty convenient.''

Rosales laughed. "Maybe, maybe not. It all depends on who we run into and what they happen to think of the governor. Governors have more enemies than friends, Ben. You know that as well as I do.''

Allison chuckled. "Hell, I guess so. Politicians is all the same, I guess, don't matter where they come from. Mexico, Washington, England. No damn difference. Only thing worse than politicians is royalty. I remember them Russians come through here a couple years back, royalty they was, had a painter along with them. They wanted to meet Indians. Drove me near crazy with their damn foolishness and questions. My God, they about wore me out. And all the time looking down their damn noses at me because I wasn't nobody. It's like they wanted the damn President to come along, wipe their asses for them. Royalty, politicians, Lord help us, they're all the same. Pack of damn fools. But it can't hurt nothing, is what I figure. So you go on along with him, see what you can find out. Maybe we'll put a stop to this damn business a whole lot sooner that I thought.''

Rosales pursed his lips thoughtfully, looked at McMasters, and asked, "When do you want to leave?''

"Sooner the better, *Señor* Rosales.''

"Call me Mike. Ben calls me that so much and so loud, it's pretty near the only thing I answer to anymore.''

Allison laughed, poured himself another drink, then fished a third glass out of his desk drawer, filled it to the brim for Rosales, and topped off Boyd's glass, which was still half full. Setting the decanter down with a crack, he lifted his glass, held it high, and said, "Here's to a hair trigger and a short rope.'' The other two men clinked their glasses, acknowledged the toast, and took a sip. Allison, though, swallowed his shot in one gulp, wiped his lips on the back of his hand, and sighed. "That stuff'll keep the termites out of your gullet, all right."

McMasters finished his drink, but Rosales set his glass, still half full, down on the desk.

"All right, now," Allison said. "You two git. But you be careful, and if you run into them rustlers, don't you try to take them on by yourself. You turn tail and git on back here. We'll round up a few of the boys and go back after them. No sense gettin' yourself killed."

"Don't worry, Ben. That's not why I came down here," Boyd said.

Miguel Rosales led the way out of the study. Once they were outside, he told McMasters to mount up and wait for him. "I'll get my own horse and I'll be right back. If you need any water to fill your canteens, there's a well behind the house."

McMasters watched him leave, wondering at the sudden coolness in the Mexican's demeanor. In Allison's study, Rosales had seemed friendly. Now there was a distance, as if he resented McMasters, or at least resented having to accompany him. But on reflection, Boyd decided that he would probably feel the same way. Rosales was the foreman, and had quite enough to deal with as it was. The Rocking A was a huge spread, and according to Allison, he employed forty men. If those men were like most cowboys, they needed somebody to ride herd on them every bit as hard as they rode herd on the livestock.

McMasters climbed into the saddle, checked his canteens, and decided he had plenty of water. As he dropped them back into place, he heard the clop of hooves approaching, and Rosales rounded the corner riding a big bay.

The foreman headed straight for the gate, leaving McMasters to follow after him. As they rode out into the open range, McMasters moved up alongside Rosales. "You speak pretty good English," he said.

"Better than your Spanish, I'll bet," Rosales answered. There was no hint of amusement in the reply. "But then, I've been here for twenty years."

"How long have you worked for Mr. Allison?"

"Twenty years. I was working for him before he married my sister. I started out as a ranch hand and worked my way up to foreman in two years."

"Have you got any ideas on what's been going on around here?"

Miguel looked at him sharply, his eyes hooded and cold. "Now, why would you think I had ideas I wouldn't have shared with Ben?"

"I didn't mean that. I just meant that sometimes we have hunches, little suspicions, things we don't feel sure about, so we keep them to ourselves."

"Maybe you do. I don't. This ranch belongs to my sister as well as to Ben. I had any suspicions, you can bet I would have done something about them. Ben's been good to me, to Carmen, and he treats me fairly, so—"

"Like a brother?"

Once more, Rosales gave him a strange look. "Yeah, like a brother," he answered. Glancing at the sky, he said. "Storm coming. We better hurry."

McMasters took that as a signal that the conversation was over for the time being. He prodded the roan into a fast trot, angled toward the southwest, and moved ahead of Rosales, aiming for a point south of San Pedro.

Looking up at the sky, McMasters realized that Rosales was right. Huge thunderheads, their tops thousands of feet in the air, flattened as if they were pressing against some invisible barrier, now boiled and churned, seeming to grow thicker and blacker even as McMasters watched. A haze covered the sun, half shielding it now and then, the rest of the time just damping its light where it floated like a bleary eye peering from behind a strip of gauze.

In fifteen or twenty minutes, as McMasters knew only too well, the sky could tear apart and let loose everything from torrential rain to hailstones the size of bird eggs, or even worse, a twister. He'd nearly been caught by a tornado once, and as long as he lived, he would never forget the frightening moan as the funnel bore down on him, dancing and feinting like a mad fencer, keeping him off balance, confusing him and terrifying his mount until finally he just leapt from the saddle into an arroyo and hugged the ground until the funnel passed. That was something he hoped he'd never experience again.

The haze was changing to an overcast, and the first tentative claps of thunder rumbled across the plains, sounding as if the distant mountains were being rearranged like furniture. He turned to look at Rosales, who was staying right on his tail.

McMasters slowed a bit, feeling the first few drops of rain spatter the backs of his hands. "You think we ought to head back?" he asked.

"Depends on how bad you want to track that herd. Chances are, all we find is tracks anyhow, and maybe not even that. The river is shallow this time of year, and if they crossed, they might have driven them cows up or downstream for a mile or more just to cover their trail. It's gonna rain buckets for certain before we get halfway there, and whatever there was to see will most likely be washed away."

As if to reinforce Miguel's assessment, a streak of lightning slashed across the boiling black clouds dead ahead, followed by the deafening explosion of a thunderclap. Immediately, the rain began in earnest, the drops kicking up puffs of dust as they slammed into the ground, and rattling like drumsticks on a snare as they pelted the brim of Boyd's hat.

Another sound, this one earsplitting, as if the sky were made of cloth and someone were tearing it in half, was followed by another thunderclap.

"That's it then," McMasters said. "We'd better head on back."

Six

After the palatial hacienda of the Rocking A ranch, the San Pedro Hotel seemed even more dilapidated. But McMasters knew he needed information, and San Pedro was the place to get it. He tied the roan out front and went up to his room, waving to the clerk, who looked questioningly at him, as if waiting for McMasters to ask him for something, more than likely another "bath."

But McMasters climbed the rickety stairs to his room and closed the door behind him with a bang that echoed all the way down the two flights of stairs to the lobby. He searched the room, looking for someplace to hide his rifle. Security at the hotel was non-existent, and he didn't want to carry the gun with him every place he went. He didn't trust the clerk, who seemed to be a little too interested in other people's business, and he didn't want to leave the gun in the boot at the livery stable. That meant he had to find someplace in the hotel room. There was a closet, but that was too obvious. Under the mattress would be more obvious still. It was the first place anyone entering the room would look for cash or other valuables.

As he paced, he listened to the creak of the floorboards,

and decided to have a look under the faded carpet. The
boards were loose, and he found one that had nail holes but
no nails. He wondered whether someone else had once had
the same idea. With the tip of his sheath knife, he pried the
board up enough to grab it with his fingers, then tugged it
free. Beneath it, he found a hollow space, but the floorboards
ran perpendicular to the beams, and with just one board free,
there wasn't enough room to maneuver the long-barreled rifle
into the opening.

McMasters tugged a second board free with a protesting
squeal from the nails, and now, with a little judicious twist-
ing and turning of the rifle, he could get it into the narrow
opening. Replacing the boards, he tugged the carpet back into
place and walked back and forth a few times, listening to the
squeak of timber on timber until he was satisfied that there
was nothing unusual in the sound of the hiding place.

Leaving his room, he went down to the lobby again. This
time, the clerk ignored him, and McMasters went out into
the street. Large puddles from the heavy rains earlier in the
day made a mess of the street. Straw floated on the muddy
water, and long-legged skimmers darted across it on their
broad, flat feet as serenely as if they were in a woodland
pond. Walking down the street, he looked for the most
crowded saloon. He wanted a chance to observe the locals a
little, keep his ears open, and just maybe pick up some useful
information.

A number of horses were hitched outside a place called
Hanrahan's Pub, and it looked as likely a place as any to suit
his purposes. As he climbed the steps up to the boardwalk,
he heard the tinkle of a piano and the subdued mutter of
drunken conversation. He pushed through the doors, his
stomach turning at the stink of sour beer. He'd been in more
than a few places like Hanrahan's in the last year and a half,
and knew that he couldn't remember half of them. Things

were different now. He could hold his liquor because, thanks to Martha, he knew when to stop. But there were times when he felt the tug. He'd get to thinking about Hannah, and he'd want to quell the pain those memories never failed to bring back.

But he walked inside, headed straight for the bar, and ordered a beer. The piano player was banging away at the keys of a battered upright, his legs pumping energetically, his shirt soaked with sweat. McMasters wondered at the devotion of a man who would pound a piano for a room of drunken men who couldn't have been less interested in what he was doing. Or maybe it wasn't devotion. Maybe it was desperation, he thought. Maybe the piano player used music the way the rest of the men in the saloon used whiskey. Maybe it was an anesthetic, something he poured on an open wound to kill some secret hurt.

The bartender was a big, ruddy-faced man with thick forearms covered with red hair. His head was less generously endowed with hair of the same color, little wisps curling around his ears and over his brow, the rest of his scalp a freckled pink expanse that showed a couple of ragged scars, probably from broken bottles. His blue eyes were clear and red-rimmed, giving him the appearance of a man who had stopped crying just a few minutes ago.

The beer in place, a silver dollar on the scarred wood, McMasters lifted the mug and turned, hooking his elbows on the bar to watch the piano player. He propped one leg up on the rail at the foot of the bar. The song was by Stephen Foster, but McMasters didn't know the title, just a few of the words, something about a girl with light brown hair. He sipped his beer slowly, letting it rest on his thigh between pulls.

McMasters scanned the crowd, thinking he might get lucky, maybe catch a glimpse of a familiar face, but of the

thirty or so men in the saloon, not one looked like Carlito
or the fat man. But they all looked familiar. All of them had
that slack-jawed look, the vacant stare, the grubby appearance of men whose lives had no horizon farther than the bar.
Some of them were playing cards, and some were talking,
their voices too loud, their laughter rough and forced. And
there were a couple, as there always were, who stared into
the foam in their mugs the way a fortune teller stared into
her tea leaves, looking for answers to questions they no
longer even remembered. McMasters had been there. He
knew what it was like to drink himself senseless, interested
in nothing and no one, using the beer or whiskey to dissolve
the hours remaining between the present and the end of their
lives.

There were no women, which was surprising, and he
thought about asking the bartender about it, then decided
against it. The door opened again, and three more men stag-
gered in, already drunk, probably just thrown out of another
saloon.

This time, he saw a familiar face. Mike Rosales was in
the center, his arms draped over the shoulders of his two
companions. It was difficult to tell whether they were
carrying him or if he was urging them inside. For an instant,
McMasters thought about calling to him, but decided that he
would bide his time, wait, and see what Rosales was up to.

The three newcomers found a table in a far corner of the
room, and when they sat down, Rosales had his back to
McMasters. One of the two men with him, both of whom
appeared to be Mexicans, stayed on his feet, tottering a little
as he listened to Rosales and the other man. They must have
been telling him what they wanted to drink, because he
turned then and made his way toward the bar, weaving uncertainly among the chair backs and crowded tables. At the
bar, he clapped his palm loudly on the damp wood, prompt-

ing an annoyed frown from the bartender, who wiped his hands on his apron, then took his sweet time walking the length of the bar.

The bartender took the order, walked slowly back in McMasters's direction, caught his eye, and rolled his own eyes heavenward, then grinned. "Some fellers can't never get enough to drink," he said. "Them fellers must have hollow legs, or something. I sure as hell don't know where they put it all."

He got a bottle of tequila, then ducked behind the bar, reappearing with a lime and a small bowl of salt. Making his way back toward the waiting Mexican, he set the bottle down, then the bowl, and dropped the lime into the salt.

The vaquero reached out to curl his fingers around the neck of the tequila bottle, scooped up the bowl, and started to turn back toward his table, but the bartender grabbed him by the arm. "Hold on, *compadre*. You got to pay first. That'll be five dollars."

The *vaquero* cursed in Spanish, set the bowl down, and fished in his pocket, coming out with several shiny coins. He let them clink one by one onto the bar, smirked, and started to leave yet again. Once more, the bartender clamped his big hand on the Mexican's shoulder. "Wait a minute, partner. Let me make sure. "I said dollars, not pesos."

Holding onto the man's arm, he gathered the coins into a mound with his thick fingers, then examined them one by one, sliding each off the top of the stack when he was satisfied with it.

The fourth one caused him to shake his head. "This is a peso, amigo, not a dollar. I don't take pesos."

"Que?"

"I said I don't take pesos. This is a peso. You got to give me a dollar. Take this one back." He flicked the peso with a fingernail, and it slid off the coin beneath it, coming to rest against the man's belly at the edge of the bar.

The Mexican looked at the coin as if he had never seen it before. He was angry, and he made no attempt to hide it. "Is good money," he said. "Silver, just like your dollars." He pointed to the pile of coins the bartender had accepted.

But the bartender was adamant. "Dollars, *compadre*, only dollars. I can't use that coin. My bank won't accept it. I won't either."

The Mexican puffed out his cheeks in exasperation and reached into his pocket, and the room was suddenly so quiet that McMasters could hear the clink of coins at the other end of the bar. The Mexican set the bottle down as he withdrew his hand, sorted through some silver in his palm, and finally scraped together the remaining dollar. He tossed the handful of small change on the bar so violently that several of the coins bounced all the way across and landed on the floor behind it.

The bartender grabbed the bottle with one hand, and bent to retrieve the coins. When they tallied, he set the bottle back down, and the Mexican immediately picked it up. "Gringo prick," the man muttered, grabbing the bowl of salt with the lime sitting in its middle. He stomped back toward the table where Rosales and the other *vaquero* were watching him.

Midway, the man tripped, spilling the salt down the back of a Texan who had started arguing with a man across the table from him. The lime plunked on the table, knocking over a glass, spilling its contents onto the deck of cards at its center. The Texan got up, the room got quiet again, and McMasters started toward the trouble, slipping easily through the motionless crowd.

He saw Rosales get up from his own table and start toward his friend. The Texan was reaching for his gun when McMasters stepped in between him and the drunken *vaquero*. "It was an accident," he said.

"I don't give a shit if it was or it wasn't. Sumbitch spilled salt down my shirt."

"It won't kill you, unless you're a slug," McMasters said.

"I don't figure this to be any of your business," the Texan snarled.

McMasters tried to calm him down. "Look, you came here to have a good time. So did everybody else. Why don't you just sit down and do that."

Rosales was at McMasters's elbow now. A quick sidelong glance showed McMasters that the Rocking A foreman was already tensing to draw his pistol, and he reached out to pat Rosales on the forearm.

"I'll buy you a drink, partner," McMasters offered.

"Don't want no drink from you." The Texan jabbed a finger at the *vaquero*. "Anybody owes me a drink, I figure it's him."

"Then *he'll* buy it," McMasters said.

Rosales spoke for the first time. "He just spent his last money at the bar. If you permit me, I'll buy it for him."

"Long as it's greaser money pays, I don't give a damn," the Texan said, starting to relax. "A real whiskey. I don't want none of that Mexican shit."

"As you wish."

The bartender had approached, and McMasters now noticed the sawed-off shotgun cradled in the crook of his right arm. He nodded to McMasters. "One whiskey," he said. "On the house. That way nobody pays, and nobody's feelings get hurt."

"Even better," the Texan said, grinning now. He waved his hand in dismissal and sat down again, reaching up to brush the salt off his shoulders.

Rosales clapped an arm around McMasters's shoulders. "Will you have a drink with me, *señor*?" he asked.

McMasters nodded.

"Let me just send my friends home while you get your drink from the bar, and you and I will have a talk, okay?" Without waiting for an answer, he moved back to his table, pushing his friend ahead of him. McMasters walked back to the bar, where the bartender was pouring the Texan's whiskey. "Thanks for that," the bartender said I don't need no shooting in here tonight. Got a bad headache as it is."

McMasters smiled. "I don't care much for the noise myself."

"Buy you a drink?"

"Already have an offer. But some other time maybe."

"You name the time, cowboy."

As McMasters walked toward Rosales's table, he saw the foreman in whispered conversation, one hand on the drunken *vaquero,* urging him toward the door. It looked as if the man was resisting leaving the saloon, but Rosales was insistent, and finally the two *vaqueros* stood up and headed for the door. McMasters sat down a moment later, and Rosales grinned. It was a distant, vacant expression without real warmth. "Sometimes the Texans and the Mexicans want to refight the Mexican War," he said. "With enough whiskey, you have a saloon full of Colonel Travises and General Santa Anas. It would be funny if people didn't get hurt so often."

Rosales poured himself a glass of tequila, downed it, and poured another. McMasters sipped his beer, then said, "Seems like tensions are pretty high around here."

Rosales snorted. "Sure they are. You got to understand. Most Texans don't have any use for Mexicans, even if the Texans were born in Kentucky or Tennessee and the Mexicans were born right here."

"You figure that's a factor in the rustling?"

Rosales shook his head. "Nope. I don't. I figure money is the only factor. But I know that Ben takes a lot of abuse from the other ranchers. They don't much like the fact that he's married to my sister. And they don't like the fact that half of our crew is Mexican. They're frustrated and they don't know where to turn. All they know to do is point a finger. That cowboy back there?''

''The one that just had his tail salted?''

Rosales nodded. ''Yeah. He works for Pete Hoffman, the Lazy H owner. I know for a fact that Hoffman thinks Ben is behind the rustling. And by Ben, he means me. But I guess it goes with the territory. I can handle it.''

McMasters was ready to leave, but Rosales coaxed him to stay for one more drink. McMasters went to the bar for another beer, and when he sat down again, he said, ''You get along with Ben all right, do you?''

Rosales gave him a strange look. ''He's my brother-in-law.'' It was delivered matter-of-factly, with no embellishment and no elaboration.

Rosales talked little after that, and McMasters was afraid that he might have offended the man. When his beer was gone, he got up again, and this time Rosales made no attempt to persuade him to stay.

Out in the street, away from the noise and the sour smell of the saloon, McMasters took his time walking back to the hotel. The clerk gave him a knowing look when he entered the lobby, but said nothing. McMasters was tired, and looked forward to a good night's sleep.

Inserting the key into the lock, he pushed the door open and sensed immediately that something was wrong. He backed away from the door, yanked out his Colt, and peered into the room from behind the door frame. Hearing nothing, he ducked inside quickly, then went to the window and pulled the curtains aside.

Dim light was all he needed to see that the place was a mess. He found the lamp, lit it, and turned the wick way up. The mattress was on the floor and his saddlebags were open, their contents dumped onto the floor beside it. His spare shirt had been torn, probably out of spite. He looked at the rug, afraid that it might have been moved, and rolled it aside, then knelt to pry open the hiding place under the floorboards. He sighed with relief when he saw the big rifle still where he'd left it.

But he'd caught someone's attention. That much was certain. The question was, whose?

Seven

Three days. Three days of sweat, dust, and unbearable heat, all combining to coat McMasters with a layer of beige plaster. He needed a break, a lead, some sort of lucky turn that would let him get a little closer to the heart of the problem. The break had come, or so he'd thought, when he'd spotted the portly Texan who had been with Carlito that first day. But it had been a dry hole. The terrain had been against him and he'd lost the fat man in less than three hours. Margarita was doing her best, but sifting through the bits of gossip she collected was as tedious as panning for gold, and not half as profitable.

So that left riding, crisscrossing the prairie like some mindless vagabond, his eye on the horizon and his nose to the ground. The mere thought of the physical contortions a literal interpretation of that activity would require was enough to give him muscle cramps.

The more he rode, the less certain he became of what it was he was looking for. And the more tempting became the idea of heading across the border. Now he was sitting under a cottonwood, its peeling bark digging into his back. The flies were persistent, their snarling buzz the perfect expression of his own mood. It was time to get back in the saddle, and as he climbed to his feet, it occurred to him that he'd have been better off if he'd been born a centaur. At least his butt wouldn't be so damned sore.

He yanked the stake pin out of the ground, gathered the tether rope into a tight coil, and draped it over his saddlehorn. Swinging up into the worn leather throne, he glanced at the horizon one more time, his eyes stinging with sweat, the bright sun threatening to burn its way through his squinting lids. And then he stopped, one leg still shy of the stirrup. He shook his head, wiped his eyes on the dusty sleeve of his shirt, and squinted once more. Dust, lots of it, not more than three miles away.

"Maybe this is it," he whispered, reaching for his field glasses. He raised them to his eyes, searched the searing blue edge of the world for a few seconds until he found the same beige smudge, this time clearly discernible for what it was, the evidence that a large group of animals was on the move. The buffalo herds were ancient history, so that left an army or a herd of livestock. There was no war on, and he knew enough about cows and horses to know that they didn't move in such numbers on their own, not unless something had stampeded them. It might be nothing, but then again it just might be the break he'd been all but praying for.

The cloud was moving southeast, away from him and away from San Pedro, but toward the Rio Grande. He knew the terrain a little better now, but there still wasn't a hell of a lot he could do about its flatness. Getting close enough to see anything worth seeing was not going to be easy. For a moment, he considered making a wide circle, getting between the cloud and the border, letting the herd, if that's what it was, come to him. But it would be harder to get close from up front. From the rear, the dust itself would offer him a little cover. The crosswind was driving the cloud in an easterly direction, and he decided to come in from the east, cloaked by the swirling beige dust.

He lashed the roan twice with the reins, then used his spurs to prod a fast trot from the big stallion. Suddenly, his energy was back. His butt no longer ached, and he forgot about the accumulated little miseries of three empty days in search of a chink in the rustlers' armor.

In fifteen minutes, he was close enough to make out the silhouettes of the wing riders on the east. They had the worst of it because the breeze, such as it was, was driving the dust right at them. He pushed the roan down over a low rise and dismounted, using the reins to hobble the horse, then snatching his binoculars from the saddle and draping them around his neck. He scooted up the side of the next low hill, dropping to his stomach when he was still a few feet from the crest. The little bowl-shaped depression behind him was no more than fifteen feet below the crest, but it was enough to conceal his mount, and that was all he wanted.

Lying flat on his stomach, he crawled the last few yards to the top of the hill and trained the glasses on the herd. This one was smaller than the one he'd stumbled across on the way into San Pedro, maybe four hundred head. He counted six drovers, but the dust was so thick he couldn't be sure he'd counted them all. Nobody seemed to be riding point, but a herd that size could be moved without a point man if absolutely necessary. It seemed they had two men on each wing, and two riding drag.

The men were almost shapeless, little more than dust devils on horseback, and there was nothing about any of them that looked remotely familiar. It was possible that it was just a handful of men driving a few hundred head to sell in Mexico, all on the up and up, but he wanted to make sure this time before anyone knew he was there.

He tried scanning the flanks of the beeves through the

glasses, but there was no way to read a brand through the boiling dust. Not at that distance. He had to get closer, but that was going to be difficult, if not impossible. For the moment, he would have to hang back, follow the herd, and hope.

He knelt there, his elation turning to a sourness in his gut, the frustration of the past few days beginning to boil up inside him. If only he knew for certain the cattle had been stolen, he would be content to trail in the wake of the herd, find where they were being taken. But it could be three or four days if the herd was heading toward Matamoros, and if the beeves *hadn't* been stolen, he would have nothing to show for his effort but ninety-six wasted hours.

A half hour later, he backed down the hill, swung into the saddle, and pushed the roan up over the crest of yet one more hill. He followed the herd for two hours, the sun hammering him remorselessly, time dragging until he thought he could spend the rest of his life on the trail and never know where he was heading or why.

And it was another hour before he got the break he was looking for. Fording a shallow creek, flanked by thick brush on both sides, he heard the bellow of an angry animal. And as he broke through the brush on the far side, he was stunned by the sudden charge of an enraged cow. The roan reared up on its hind legs so abruptly it nearly tumbled McMasters from the saddle. The cow charged to within ten feet and stopped, backing away now, wary of the roan's slashing hooves.

At first, McMasters was confused, but as the cow backed off, it turned, and he saw then a calf, sick, down on its knees. The cow must have been its mother. It moved in close enough to nudge the calf with its nose. The calf tried to get to its feet, but its legs would not hold it. They buckled again, and the calf went down. Once more the cow tried to nudge it into motion, and once more the calf tried.

McMasters watched, fascinated, and he held the roan in check, backing toward the brush until its rump broke through again. He could hear the trickle of water running over stones behind him, the frustrated breathing of the cow, and now the bleat of the calf, obviously frightened, obviously suffering.

The cow turned again to look at him, then maneuvered itself to a position where it could nudge the calf and watch the interlopers at the same time. It was then that McMasters noticed the brand burned into the cow's flank. It was the Rocking A of Ben Allison.

The calf was prostrate now, its legs folded beneath it, its head resting on the grass. Its eyes kept closing, and the mother kept poking at it, trying to force it to its feet. But it was obvious the calf was finished, not just exhausted, but dying. It was something that happened hundreds of times a day, but something McMasters had never thought about. He could sense the cow's desperation, sense too its inability to understand what was happening. It did the only thing it knew to do, but the calf was beyond saving.

Without thinking, McMasters drew his Colt .44 and thumbed back the hammer. For a long moment, he thought about putting the calf out of its misery, vaguely conscious that the gunshot would alert the cattle drovers up ahead, but not caring. He actually brought the gun up and drew a bead before he realized that he was about to interfere in something that could not have been less his business. As if somehow aware of what he was thinking, the cow snorted, turned its gaze full upon him, and snorted again. The calf too seemed suddenly aware of him, its eyes fluttering open for a few moments. McMasters stared into the liquid brown and lost himself for a moment. He felt like a man who had suddenly fallen into a bottomless pool of dark water.

Then, again without thinking, he lowered the hammer and

holstered the Colt. Nature had to take its course. They were only dumb beasts, but that didn't give him the right to intervene. He jerked the reins and clucked to the roan, kicking it into a quick trot and leaving the cow and its dying calf behind. He didn't look back.

A half mile later, he slowed, conscious that he was getting too close, and that was when he heard the hoofbeats. He turned then, saw three men closing on him at a full gallop, and realized they had their guns drawn. He thought for a moment that he was imagining things, but then he saw the puff of smoke from one pistol, and an instant later heard the crack of the first shot. The charging cowboys were still well out of pistol range, and even an ordinary rifle would have been hard pressed to reach him with any certainty. The cowboys were still nearly five hundred yards away.

He reached for his rifle and dismounted, knowing that the horse made an uncertain shooting platform. Somehow they had spotted him and circled in behind him. But however it had happened, he was going to have to deal with it.

He dropped to one knee and drew a bead with the big .70-caliber rifle, calculating the windage and reaching up to adjust the rear sight. McMasters had the lead man beaded, and smiled grimly, knowing what lay in store for him. Gently, he squeezed the trigger, and felt the big rifle butt slam into his shoulder at the same instant he heard the thunderous crack.

He saw the explosion of flesh and bone as the doctored bullet struck home. Then the lead rider exploded backward off his horse. The two men on his flanks charged on for several strides, but they were looking back at their fallen companion. McMasters knew what was going through their minds. It was an impossible shot for anything but a buffalo gun, but it was not likely they had ever seen a Sharps or a

Spencer in action, at least not in the hands of a man who really knew how to use it.

They jerked their mounts to a halt and dismounted. One of the men, in a crouch, sprinted back to the fallen cowboy, and McMasters chambered another shell. He watched as the the cowboy bent over his fallen colleague, then recoiled. McMasters almost laughed as he tried to visualize the stunned disbelief on the cowboy's face. The .70-caliber bullet would have fragmented on impact, and torn a huge hole in the chest and back of the dead man, for he was surely that.

McMasters aimed again, but the cowboy suddenly regained his senses and dove to the ground. McMasters could hear him calling to the other man, kneeling beside his horse, but the men were too far away for him to make out what was being said. Taking one of them alive would have been useful, but McMasters didn't see how he could manage it. He couldn't get close enough without shooting them both first, and neither one of them would have been breathing by the time he closed the few hundred yards between himself and his targets.

He knelt there watching them, waiting to see whether they would stand and fight or if they would back away. The closer man fired once, lying on his stomach and using his pistol, but the pathetic little crack of the handgun was all but lost on the hot wind. The man started to crawl toward his mount, grazing a few yards away, and McMasters knew what he was doing. He drew a bead on the side of the horse and waited, knowing the man was going for his rifle.

A moment later, the figure of the cowboy bobbed into view, and McMasters pulled the trigger once more. Again the big rifle boomed, and once more the bullet found its target, not the man, but his horse. The animal, a sturdy little chestnut quarter horse, went down as if felled by a poleax between the eyes, and the man dove over the saddle to take cover behind the brand-new carcass.

McMasters saw the glint of a rifle barrel as the cowboy yanked his repeater from its boot. His own horse was behind him, not an easy shot even for a marksman, but there was the chance that a stray bullet might catch the roan. McMasters turned, and had started toward the roan when he spotted movement on the far side of the horse. He ducked to one side, and saw four men charging full tilt toward him.

"Damn!" Either they had heard the gunfire, or this had been the plan all along, to pincer him. They'd backshoot him if they could get close enough, and if not, they'd have him surrounded and it would just be a matter of time. They could wait him out all day, if it took that long, and after sundown they could get a whole lot closer. If that happened, the advantage of the big rifle was gone. It might as well be hand-to-hand combat. He had the same deadly ammunition for his Colt revolver, but he had to be able to see to use it.

Dropping to his knees again, he took aim on the lead rider and squeezed off a quick shot. He saw the man grab his shoulder as he slid from the saddle, but didn't wait to see anything else. He vaulted onto the roan and kicked it hard, slamming the rifle into its scabbard and heading east. They could fall in behind him if they wanted to. He would be more than happy to exchange shots at long range. But something told him that wasn't about to happen.

He rode flat out for half a mile, turning to glance over his shoulder now and then. The men were on his tail, but they seemed to have little taste for the chase. They were gradually falling back, either wary of the big rifle, or satisfied that they had driven him off.

He had made contact, but that was cold comfort. He still had no idea where the cattle were being taken, and he hadn't gotten a clear look at any of the rustlers. But at least he had them thinking, and that was a start.

Eight

McMasters lay on the bed, the window open against the heat. He had the curtain pulled back to let in a breeze, but the bunched cloth was not moving at all. It was late, nearly midnight. Restless, he sat up, let his bare feet hit the floor, and walked to the window, where he knelt and propped his elbows on the sill. He could hear the raucous sounds of the saloons, the tinny clatter of the town's only piano. There was a time when the noise would have drawn him like the flicker of a candle flame drew a moth. But that time was well behind him now.

Thinking of Martha Blair, he smiled. She would be smiling too if she could see him, sharing his satisfaction at having crawled out of the bottle once and for all. And there would be a hint of flirtation too in that smile. Martha had a way of knowing how to get under his skin when she thought he was being stubborn or stupid, and she had a way of moving that was seductive without trying to be. He missed her. He missed the smell of her, that clean, fresh-scrubbed hint of brown soap that clung to her, and the scent of honeysuckle that seemed to surround her, wafting toward him with every cant of a hip or swirl of her skirt. He missed too the feel of her, the weight of a breast in his callused palm, the soft down of her arms, the ripple of muscle under his fingers as he stroked her back or caressed a thigh.

The thing he missed most, though, was her sense of herself. She was self-contained, complete without him. She did not cling to him, or try to smother him. She simply was herself, with him or without him. Simply put, she did not need him, and did not try to pretend otherwise. And because she did not need him, he wanted her all the more.

There had been other women since he'd met Martha, and she did not mind. There had not been many, and they had not mattered much really, the passion, if it could even be called that, as momentary as mayflies. He was not certain, but suspected that there had been other men for her too since they'd met. And he preferred that uncertainty. He did not know how he would feel if he learned that she was as independent as she had taught him to be. But he knew she would not apologize, nor would she tolerate any suggestion of possessiveness or jealousy. "I am who and what I am," she would say, "Just as you are, and you have no right to expect me to be any different. You don't, after all, own me, Boyd McMasters."

Then she would smile, her lower lip pouting just a little, and she would crook a finger and start to unbutton her dress. And he would forget all about everything but Martha before that dress ever hit the floor.

Shaking his head, he got to his feet, trying to ignore the drunken shouts from the next block. He walked back to the bed and sat down, propping an elbow on his knee and resting his chin in the open palm of his right hand. He remembered what it had been like a year and a half before, when he had been driven, so hellbent on revenge that there was not a minute he had not been in restless motion, except for those times he'd drunk himself into a stupor, his senses pickled, his body numb to everything, his mind number still.

But his thirst for vengeance had been slaked. The blood of the Winslow clan had satisfied it. Now, he was able to go about his business with a sense of purpose, a belief that he was making decisions rather than following some law as old as the Bible, whether he wished to or not. And yet he still felt frustrated, cheated somehow. Without realizing it, he had pursued the Winslows in the belief that once they were dead and buried, the world would be a better place, perhaps even a just place. It had not mattered to him whether he survived the process, so long as it succeeded. Now, he realized that he had been deluding himself. Winslows were a dime a dozen, common as clay, numberless as ants or bees or blades of grass.

Evil had as many heads as the Hydra. Cut one off, and two grew back. Cut them off and four took their place. It was tempting to think that if you stopped, let well enough alone, things would get no worse. Tempting, but unrealistic, and Boyd McMasters knew it. You had to keep cutting and slashing, because those heads kept growing no matter what you did.

He wanted a Primero, that cheap, even disgusting little cigarillo he had come to favor, but he was fresh out, and they were hard to come by. He'd have to settle for a hand-rolled cigarette, and reached for his tobacco pouch and loosened the drawstrings. He opened a cigarette paper, and had just started to tap the tobacco into it when he heard a soft knock on the door. Not expecting anyone, he snatched at his gunbelt, hanging on a chair beside the bed. He drew the Colt and thumbed back the hammer before padding to the door in his bare feet.

Again the knock came, this time a little louder, a little more insistent.

"Who is it?" he asked.

"Margarita, *señor*. Please, you have to help."

Holding the Colt ready at his waist, he unlatched the door and pulled it open.

Margarita burst inside. She was crying, her cheeks red and puffy, a gray blue smear on her left cheek which it took him a moment to realize was a bruise just beginning to form.

"What is it, Margarita? What's wrong?"

"You have to come, *señor*. Come now. You have to . . ."

McMasters looked down at his legs, encased in long underwear, and nodded. He ran back to the bed and snatched at his jeans. Sitting down to draw them on, he asked again, "What's wrong?"

"It is a man. He is beating Guadalupe. He will kill her, *señor*, if you don't help."

Tugging on his boots, he tamped them in place and draped the gunbelt around his waist. "Come on," he said. "Show me where."

Margarita sniffled once, then said, "Thank you, Señor Boyd." She turned then and ran out the door. He was right on her heels, his boots thudding on the worn carpet, and followed Margarita down the two flights of stairs and into the lobby. She raced for the front door and burst into the street. McMasters was much taller, and he had to slow up a little to avoid running right past her.

"Where are we going?" he asked. But Margarita shook her head, and he followed mutely in her wake.

Two blocks down the street, she turned left and pointed to an adobe building. It sported a faded sign that said "Cantina," but as far as McMasters knew, it was no longer in business. Margarita pointed. "In there, *Señor* Boyd. In back."

McMasters didn't wait for her now. He broke into a sprint. As he closed on the front of the building, he heard a high-pitched shriek, then the angry snarl of a man obviously drunk. "Bitch, I'll cut your heart out," the man shouted.

McMasters reached the building, raced to its left end, and down alongside the cracked adobe walls. He saw light through a window covered with dark red curtains. The window was open, and he could hear plainly now the steady thump of flesh on flesh, the man grunting with every blow, the woman moaning now, either too hurt or too exhausted to bother screaming any longer.

Turning the corner, he found the door, a makeshift affair of wooden planks opened with a drawstring. He jerked the string so hard it snapped, and he could no longer operate the latch. The woman screamed once more, this time a long, piercing shriek that ended in a shuddering moan, and McMasters hurled himself against the planks. They were dry and brittle, and the latch burst open at once, spilling Mc-Masters into the room, He saw now that the light too was red, a lamp with a shade of some sort of red cloth attached to its chimney.

The man looked up in surprise, his fist poised above his head in preparation for delivering yet another punch.

"Get the hell out of here, cowboy. This don't concern you," he muttered. He turned threateningly, and McMasters saw the woman shrink away, pushing with her legs against the drunken man's hip. He was big, thick through the middle, his bare chest speckled with rubies where the red light reflected from drops of sweat. Even his black hair had a ruby sheen from the glistening hair oil.

The woman was naked, and McMasters felt vaguely embarrassed, as much for himself as for her, as if he had burst in out of some misplaced urge to snoop. The man turned back to business and bent over the woman, but McMasters leaped at him, catching the upraised fist as it was about to descend. The man grunted in surprise and cursed in a rage. "Bastard, I warned you." He slapped his hip, forgetting that he had removed his gunbelt. McMasters saw it on the floor beside the bed.

As the slight flicker of McMasters's gaze reminded him, he jerked free and reached for the gun, but McMasters yanked his Colt and brought it down hard on the back of the cowboy's skull. The sharp crack of steel on the bony ridge sounded like a stout tree limb snapping in two, and the man fell to his knees, grunting like a rooting pig but still conscious. He reached for the back of his head, yelped when his fingers grazed the welt, and when he saw blood on his fingertips, he cursed again. McMasters delivered a sudden kick, catching the man under the chin with the toe of his boot and snapping the bully's head back sharply.

The woman screamed again as the drunk collapsed across her legs, and she covered her breasts with both arms folded over her naked chest, while kicking viciously at the man with both bare feet.

McMasters grabbed the man by the ankles and dragged him off the bed, not batting an eye when the man's head slammed into the dirt floor of the old cantina with the sound of a ripe melon bursting. The man groaned once, but made no attempt to free himself from the iron grip on his naked ankles.

McMasters hauled him to the front door, only then realizing that Margarita was standing there, her hands to her mouth. Even in the dim red light, he could see her eyes wide with fear. The bruise took on color from the lamp, and looked more prominent than it had in the lamplight of his own room.

Margarita craned her neck to look past McMasters, then darted in around him to begin ministering to her friend. Hauling the drunk outside, McMasters dumped him unceremoniously in a heap, then went back inside, picked up the man's gunbelt, removed the Colt Peacemaker from the holster, and

tucked it into his own belt. Then he walked to the doorway
and tossed the gunbelt into the street. The man's boots followed, along with the rest of his clothing, which McMasters
tossed into a nearby horse trough.

When he returned, Guadalupe was slipping into a dress,
and Margarita was helping her button it.

"Are you all right, *señorita?*" McMasters asked.

"*Sí, señor.* Thank you." Guadalupe smiled at him, then
fussed with her hair, trying to shape it with both hands, as
if her appearance were of concern to him.

McMasters could see that her face was badly bruised, her
lower lip swollen, her upper lip split in two places, and one
eye beginning to blacken and close. Both bare shoulders bore
the white imprints of fingers outlined in red where the man
had squeezed her brutally with both hands. Margarita went
to a small table in one corner, and came back with a wet
cloth and a pitcher of water. She started to dab at the bruises
on Guadalupe's cheeks, but they hurt too much even for so
tender a touch, and she was forced to stop.

"You'd better put her to bed, Margarita," McMasters
said.

The young woman nodded, pressed her friend backward
to the bed, and held on while Guadalupe lowered herself to
the rustling pallet under its layer of blankets.

McMasters spotted a bottle of whiskey on the night table,
and walked over to get it. A small cup sat beside it, and he
pulled the cork, poured some whiskey into the tin cup, and
restoppered the bottle. He walked back to the bed, where
Guadalupe was trying to slip out of her dress again. The
blanket slid away, and her breasts were bare. McMasters, in
spite of himself, admired their ripeness, and Guadalupe, true
to her instincts, smiled and tried to wink. "You come back
when I look better, *señor,* and I will thank you properly."

"I just might do that, *señorita,*" McMasters said, grinning. It even seemed like a good idea, but Margarita scowled at him, and he stopped smiling.

"Who was he?" McMasters asked, changing the subject to less sensitive matters.

"A pig, *señor,*" Guadalupe said, "A drunken pig, who thinks because I am a *puta* he can do what he wants to me."

"Well, I don't think he'll be bothering you again any time soon."

"Did you kill him, *señor?*" The question was full of hope, and when McMasters shook his head no, Guadalupe pouted. "Too bad," she said. "Maybe you should have. He is one of the ones you want."

"What?" He looked at Margarita, who nodded.

Guadalupe patted the pallet beside her hip. "Sit down, *señor,* and I will tell you what I know."

Again he looked at Margarita, almost as if asking her permission, and when she gave her approval, he lowered himself to the pallet. His weight made the ancient springs beneath it whine in protest, and as Guadalupe shifted around to look him in the eye, her breasts once more peeked out from under the blanket. Her battered face wore a mischievous smile, and McMasters leaned over to brush his lips against her forehead, tugging the blanket back into place as he did so. "Tell me, *señorita,*" he said. "Tell me what you know."

"You are looking for the men who steal the cows, no? Margarita told me this, and asked me to try to hear things. And this is what I did."

"And that pig outside is one of the rustlers, Guadalupe?"

"*Sí, señor.* I know him well. He comes to me all the time, and he likes to talk, especially when he gets drunk. Sometimes he gets rough, and then . . ." She shrugged. "But he always pays. He gets the money when they take the cows to Mexico. Then he comes back to see me."

"Who is he? Where does he work?"

She shrugged. "They call him Wilson. That is all I know about that. And he works only stealing the cows. But I know where he stays when he is not doing that or drinking up his pesos. There is a little town in Tamaulipas called Las Palomas, on the Rio San Juan. There are many men there who do this thing. You should not look into this thing, *señor*. They have powerful friends on both sides of the river."

"I have powerful friends too, Guadalupe." He patted the Colt on his hip, and smiled coldly.

Nine

For the last mile, the brilliant white tiles that spelled out the Rocking A brand on the roof of the Allison hacienda glittered in the sun like some sort of sign from heaven. McMasters felt at long last that he was finally getting somewhere.

Guadalupe had told him more—not the complete picture, but he couldn't expect that. But he had learned enough to see the general outlines of the problem facing him. He wanted to talk to Allison, see if what he learned explained anything the old Ranger might know. And he was hoping that maybe Miguel Rosales could add a few new pieces to the puzzle.

Allison was just dismounting in front of his house when McMasters passed under the arch at the main gate. The older man turned to see who was coming, leaving one foot in a stirrup, resting his arm across the saddle. As McMasters drew close enough to be recognized, Allison put his foot down and took off his hat to wave it overhead.

McMasters rode up to the hitching post and prepared to dismount, Allison waiting impatiently beside the big roan. "Didn't expect to see you back here so soon, Boyd," he said. "You got any news?"

"Might could be," McMasters answered, swinging down from the saddle. "I don't know whether it means anything or not. I was hoping we could talk about it a little. Then I thought maybe we could take a ride out, look at your herds, talk to some of your men."

"Sure, sure thing. Let's go on inside first. You had breakfast yet?"

McMasters nodded. "Yep."

"Well, I need a cup of coffee. Join me?"

McMasters shrugged. "All right."

"We can talk in the kitchen, save a little time," Allison added.

The big rancher led the way into the lavish house. He seemed completely unself-conscious, as if his obvious wealth were neither extraordinary nor reason for embarrassment. McMasters couldn't help but compare the way Allison lived to the way he himself had lived when he had had roots and a place he called home. He could still see in his mind's eye the modest frame home, the light in the window he had taken for a lantern, and as his boots thumped on the polished floor, the picture in his memory burst into flame and he could hear once more the screams as Hannah fought to get free of the ropes binding her to the bed.

He was used to the memories, but they still made his blood run cold, and he tried to stop his ears against the awful screams. They took him out of himself, and he could look down on the scene, watching as he clawed at the doors, smashed in the windows, driven back at every turn by the ravenous flames until the roof caved in with a thunderous roar that left him empty, except for the ringing in his ears.

Martha had told him it would never change, but that he would learn how to handle it better. The pain would not go away, she'd told him, but it would grow dull, become an ache instead of a stab. But so far, the change was slow in coming. He usually lost concentration during these episodes, and did so now.

Allison reached out and shook him by the arm, snapping him rudely back to the present. "You all right, old son?"

McMasters nodded. "Yeah, I'm fine."

"Thought you'd gone south on me there for a minute."

McMasters shook his head, partly to contradict Allison and partly to chase away the last searing remnants of recollection. "Just a little preoccupied," he said.

They were in the kitchen, and Allison snatched a big blackened coffee pot from the stove and a pair of mugs from a shelf. He poured both cups full, and had turned to head back to the stove when someone asked, "Where's mine?"

Both men turned to see Rosalita Allison standing in the doorway. Dressed in jeans and checkered shirt that did little to conceal the lush figure beneath it, she brushed past McMasters, walked to the shelf, and grabbed a cup for herself. She watched as Allison filled it, then got some sugar from a bowl on the table and added three spoonfuls to the swirling black liquid, stirring it so vigorously, a little coffee spilled onto the table.

"You men are always drinking this awful stuff straight," she said, winking at McMasters.

Allison spluttered, "If it's so godawful, what are you drinking it at all for?"

"Just to prove that I'm as good as any man on this ranch."

Allison shook his head, then dropped heavily into a chair, patted the table for McMasters to join him, and said, "Honey, there ain't a man on this spread who doesn't already know that. You make it plain about a hundred times a day."

"Mr. McMasters doesn't know," she answered, smiling at the visitor but keeping an eye on her father. She took her own seat, and pulled the cup close, curling her hands around it and leaning forward to sniff the swirling steam.

Allison took a sip of his coffee, then looked at McMasters. "So, what brings you out here?"

"Couple things. Yesterday, I ran across another small herd being driven toward the border. I trailed it for a while, long enough to learn that at least some of the beeves were yours."

"Mine? How do you know?"

McMasters told him about the calf and the brand on the mother, then went on. "I was staying with them, figured I'd follow them as far as I could, but they tumbled to it, and somebody jumped me. Had to shoot one of them."

"Not the same ones you tangled with the other day, was they?"

McMasters shook his head uncertainly. "Can't be sure. But there's more. Ever hear of a place called Las Palomas?"

Allison pursed his lips in thought. "Nope, can't say as I have. North of the border, is it?"

"No. Down in Tamaulipas. Fifteen, twenty miles from Reynosa, it's supposed to be. On the Rio San Juan."

"Nope. It don't ring a bell."

"Uncle Miguel would know it, I bet," Rosalita suggested.

Allison looked at her sternly. "Honey, me and Mr. McMasters got some serious business to talk about. You want to stay at the table, that's fine, but try not to interrupt, won't you?"

Rosalita pouted. "Just trying to help, Papa."

"Just hush up. That would be a big help."

Rosalita looked to MacMasters for support, giving him a radiant smile and reaching out to touch him on the wrist. "I'm sorry," she said. "I just thought maybe I could be useful." She squeezed the wrist, and McMasters felt a tingle that he didn't want to feel. Not here, not now.

"Where'd you come by this information, Boyd?" Allison asked.

The question made McMasters uncomfortable. He looked at Rosalita, and decided he'd rather she not know, so he shrugged and said, "Askin' around, here an there. Little bits and pieces all sort of came together."

"And what exactly is it that you've learned?" Rosalita asked.

"There is supposed to be some sort of camp near Las Palomas. Rustlers use it as a base. They come up north, run off a few hundred head, and run 'em back across the river. That's about all I know. I don't know exactly where the camp is. I don't know how many men. I don't know where they sell the stolen beeves. But I'll sure as hell find out."

The curse made him look at Rosalita again, who grinned. "I've heard Papa say lots worse than that, Mr. McMasters." Again she touched him on the arm, this time letting her fingers linger on the bare skin below his rolled sleeve, their tips teasing the hair into curls before she withdrew her hand.

He looked at Allison, half expecting the big man to be scowling at him, but Allison was lost in thought. "Might be we should go on out and talk to the men, like you said. Some of my boys are Mexicans. They might know something."

McMasters swallowed hard before asking his next question. It was bound to be touchy, but it had to be asked. "You trust them? The Mexicans, I mean?"

Allison looked him square in the eye. "You know any reason I ought not?"

McMasters answered with a shake of his head.

"You sound more than a little like some of the other ranchers around here." Allison was annoyed now, and he didn't care who knew it.

Rosalita spoke up. "Some of the other big ranchers want Papa to fire the *vaqueros.* They think there's some connection between them and the stolen cattle."

Glad for the diversion, McMasters shifted his attention to

Rosalita. "But you don't think so?"

"I don't know. Mexicans are people, just like everybody else. There could be. But then, it could be Texans. Nobody knows."

McMasters thought back to the herd he'd encountered on the way in to San Pedro that first day. Of the dozen or so men, it looked as if most were Texans. But there were Mexicans too. He'd never gotten close enough to the men who'd jumped him the day before to see them clearly. If he'd had the telescopic sight, he'd have had a better idea, but that was spilled milk.

"All right, let's go talk to the men then," McMasters said.

"It's roundup time, or a lot of the boys would be around the bunkhouse," Allison said.

"That's all right. I wouldn't mind taking a look at your spread anyhow."

"I'm going too," Rosalita announced, in a tone that made it clear she would brook no opposition. She got up, took a sip of her coffee, and headed for the door.

"What are you going to do?" Allison asked. "She's as headstrong as her mother. There's not a chance in hell she'll stay home, unless I tie her up."

"She won't be in the way," McMasters said, wondering whether it was true, but knowing that he would enjoy her company either way.

Allison swallowed the rest of his coffee and walked around the table to clap McMasters on the shoulder. "Unless I miss my guess, that little gal has her eye on you, Boyd."

McMasters swallowed hard. "I didn't notice," he lied.

Allison laughed. "Well, I sure as hell did. And I'll tell you what, if she sets her cap for somethin', she usually gets it. You better be careful, or she'll sneak up on you with a branding iron." He laughed heartily, and McMasters blushed.

The big rancher led the way toward the front of the house, and when they stepped onto the veranda, Rosalita was already in the saddle. "What took you two so long?" she demanded.

"I was just tellin' Boyd here that he better watch his rear end, less'n you decide to lasso him and put a big R on his butt."

"Papa!"

"You're thinkin' about it, girl. Don't tell me you're not."

McMasters tried to ignore the banter, and walked off the veranda to the roan and climbed aboard.

"Don't you pay any attention to him, Boyd," Rosalita said. "He just likes to tease."

McMasters nodded, but he couldn't help but notice that she had switched to his first name and it had a kind of easy familiarity on her tongue. He found himself thinking of Martha, wondering what she would tell him to do. But he already knew, and he wasn't sure it was such a good idea.

They had to ride nearly five miles before they found the chuck wagon. Two fires nearby were stacked with branding irons, and a makeshift pen was being used to hold the calves. As Allison rode up, Miguel Rosales, who was overseeing the work, waved his hat, said something to a cowhand sitting on a chestnut stallion beside him, then rode over to greet his boss.

"What brings you out here, Ben?" he asked.

"Boyd thinks he's got a lead on the rustlers."

Rosales scowled at McMasters, but responded to Allison with a question. "So what's he doing here? He think we're the rustlers?"

Allison laughed. "Not hardly. But we thought it might be a good idea to ask the boys a few questions."

"What kind of questions?" Once more, Rosales tossed a sidelong scowl at McMasters.

"You ever hear of a place called Las Palomas, Miguel?" McMasters asked.

The Mexican shrugged. "Hell, there are probably fifty places with that name. Some dirt farmer puts up a shack, thinks he's starting a town, and doesn't know what to name it. He looks up, sees a couple of doves, and that's it—Las Palomas."

"You know of a town with that name on the Rio San Juan, down in Tamaulipas?"

Rosales shook his head. "No. But that don't mean there isn't one. Look, I got work to do. You want a lesson in geography, you get it someplace else."

"Hold on, Mike. McMasters is just trying to help."

"Don't need help."

"You could have fooled me, Rosales," Boyd snapped.

Rosales didn't answer. He jerked the reins, wheeled his horse, and spurred it, leaving a cloud of dust in his wake as he rode back to the holding pen.

McMasters was puzzled. He looked at Allison, who shook his head. "Don't mind Mike. He gets that way every roundup. Wants things to go just right, and he's pissy as hell until it's over and done with."

McMasters nodded. He wasn't so sure it was that simple, but he held his tongue.

Ten

McMasters found the trail without difficulty. Four or five hundred head of cattle leave a pretty clear impression of their passage. It made sense, he thought, to follow the trail of the rustled stock because he might stumble on something useful on the way to the river. Once he crossed the Rio, though, he would have a decision to make, whether to follow the stolen herd or to head straight for Las Palomas.

South of San Pedro, he spotted a trio of buzzards wheeling in the sky, and he remembered the calf. More than likely the birds were making ready to pick it clean. The wonder was that it hadn't aready been stripped to the bone.

A few hundred yards from the creek where he'd seen the dying calf, he found smears of blood on the dry grass and dismounted. As near as he could judge, this was the spot where the rustlers had found out what the big .70 could do. He saw scuff marks where the body had been dragged a few feet, more than likely to be hoisted onto a horse. The blood was dark, already partly covered with a layer of beige dust. Something shiny caught his eye, and when he snatched it from the grass, he realized it was a sliver of bone blasted from the shoulder, probably the shoulder blade. He turned the bone sliver over in his fingers while he watched the buzzards drop closer to the ground.

For a few seconds, he was forced to wonder about what it was he did for a living. At the moment, it seemed that his entire life was focused on killing. That the men he killed deserved it was not in doubt. That it was something he ought to be doing was less certain.

He saw one of the buzzards glide lower, then tuck its wings until it was just a few feet off the ground, when they spread wide to brake for the landing. "That's what I do," he thought. "I feed the goddamned buzzards." He tossed the bone sliver into the air and snatched at it, the way a man might toss a lucky coin, pinched the bone between his finger and thumb, then let it fall to the grass, where he ground it under his heel and crushed it into the soil until he could no longer see it.

With a sigh, he climbed back on the roan and headed for the creek. He crossed at almost the same place as before, and as the roan poked through the brush, the buzzard squawked and spread its wings, beating them angrily for a moment until it waddled away and twisted its ugly, bald head around to stare at him from the beadiest eyes this side of a rattler, waiting to see what he would do.

McMasters saw the carcass of the calf, already half stripped, and the stink drifting toward him on the hot breeze made his stomach churn. He kicked the roan and moved on, the buzzard giving him one last scolding squawk as he rode by.

Far to the south, he saw more buzzards, and wondered if they had been drawn by another dead calf. But it was on his way, and he would find out soon enough. He rode easily, not pushing the roan, trying to preserve its energy. Las Palomas wasn't going anywhere, after all.

The buzzards up ahead suddenly sailed off, soaring high,

as if they had decided to forget about whatever it was they'd been watching. Maybe, he thought, whatever it was hadn't been dead after all. The big scavengers would watch a prospective meal, sometimes for hours, waiting for the last flicker of life to disappear. But sometimes they were fooled, and a tentative approach would rouse the intended victim to one last desperate flurry of activity, and the birds would back off. There was no shortage of death, and no lack of meals for them, on the inhospitable expanse of the plains.

As he drew close to the river, twenty miles west of McAllen, he started to feel a sense of urgency, and pushed the roan harder. It was late afternoon, but it was still scalding hot, and he was anxious to get across the border, find someplace to rest. According to Guadalupe, Las Palomas was only a few miles on the far side of the river. He'd make the crossing, then head west until he found the Rio San Juan. From there, Las Palomas was a hop, skip and jump. Finding it, though, was not as much of a problem as what he would do when he got there.

He could see the river now, and the sky was filled with white birds, probably gulls heading inland, not knowing, or perhaps not caring, that there was a difference between the Gulf and the river. The terrain was barren, in places even arid. Clumps of cacti and bunch grass studded the sandy soil, and it looked as if nothing else was alive for fifty miles in any direction.

McMasters was on a bluff overlooking the sluggish sweep of the Rio Grande before he saw a small lizard bounce across the hot sand and scurry under a rock, only to back out followed by an angry rattler. He had to ride nearly a mile before he found a way to get down, and when he pushed the roan over the edge and onto the sandy slope, he had to lean back in the saddle, giving the big stallion its head on the treacherous footing.

At the edge of the river, he hesitated. This was a big step. He hadn't been working for the Cattleman's Protective Association all that long, and as far as he knew, he wasn't supposed to go into to Mexico. But that was where the stolen stock was being taken, and he had no choice but to follow.

A gentle slope ended in a sandy flat. He could see layers of sand where the river at flood had etched the dune-like mounds, and as the roan picked its way toward the water's edge, the ground crumbled under its hooves.

The river was nearly a quarter mile wide, but it was running slowly, and there was no hint of a deep channel where the current would have been swift with the surface smooth and glassy. The roan waded in, and McMasters pulled out the big .70 and held it high. The rifle was one of a kind, and he was not about to expose it to the sand-laden waters of the river. It would take him an hour to clean it after the crossing.

He was halfway across when he turned and looked back at the Texas side, wondering if he would ever see it again. The water was halfway up the stirrups now, and his boots were full, his socks sopping, but he wanted to make sure he kept a firm grip on the roan and refused to lift his feet out of the current.

The footing seemed fairly secure. The water was clear, and he could see the sandy bottom, a few fish darting around the roan's hooves to see what the disturbance was, then darting away again, their scales flashing bright blue, orange, and red in the transparent flood. Already, the water was receding as the roan climbed toward the far side, and in five minutes, McMasters nudged the big stallion up the far bank and toward the top of a low hill, where he dismounted. Rebooting the rifle, he sat down to tug off his boots and empty the water, leaving a pair of puddles on the beige soil.

He took off his socks, twisted them, and draped them across his saddle, then did the same with his jeans, nearly tying them in knots until he'd squeezed most of the water out of them. Spreading his pants and socks out on some sagebrush to dry, he got some jerked beef from his saddlebags, and sat down on the sand with his canteen in his lap for a lunch that, while anything but satisfying, at least took the edge off his hunger.

In the brilliant sun, his clothes dried quickly, and the sand was hot under his bare feet as he chewed the last of the beef and tiptoed to the brush for his pants and socks. They were still damp, but they could dry in the saddle. His boots were still sopping wet, but that couldn't be helped. As he dressed again, he watched the roan tug at some clumps of grass, then walk back down to the river for a drink. McMasters had to stamp his feet to get the damp socks to slide down into the boots. Then he walked down to the roan and climbed into the saddle.

As near as he could figure, he still had a good ten or fifteen miles to go. It was nearly that far to the Rio San Juan, which flowed north into the Rio Grande, and then he had to follow it upstream until he found Las Palomas. Once there, he could ask discreetly about the camp Guadalupe had told him about. As in San Pedro, he would rely on the predictable habits of cowboys and whores, finding a cantina or a whorehouse where he could gather the information he needed.

Back in the saddle, and up the hill, he looked south, where Mexico stretched for a thousand miles and more toward South America. He wondered that anyone would want to live in so godforsaken a place, knowing at the same time that he was being unfair. The part of Texas he'd just left behind was no more hospitable than Tamaulipas. It made him feel small, looking up at the sky and thinking that he was the only moving speck on the face of the earth.

Nearly an hour later, he saw smears of green on the western horizon, and knew it had to mean water. And in this part of Mexico, water could mean only one thing, a river. Twenty minutes later, he struck the Rio San Juan.

The San Juan was like a miniature version of the Rio Grande, its banks greener by a little, mostly with brush and grass. A few stunted trees, scrub oak and elder mostly, stood guard over the sluggish current, but the climate was just too harsh for the thick foliage and the dense stands of trees more northerly rivers supported on their banks.

He stayed on the east bank and headed south, knowing that he was in the homestretch. He reached Las Palomas, or so the battered signboard staked in the sand claimed, about an hour later. It was San Pedro Mexican-style, a couple of blocks long and a couple of blocks wide, built around a central plaza, the architecture primarly a functional version of the adobe Ben Allison had used for his home. And in keeping with the Mexican way, the town's centerpiece was its Catholic church, a white spire stabbing at the sky as if to get God's attention.

The baked clay of most of the buildings had been allowed to crack, and only a handful of them had seen even minimal maintenance in a dozen years or more.

One of them, whitewashed, had a sign nailed to the lintel over its front door identifying it in Spanish as "Pedro's Cantina." Under the neat black lettering, someone, probably a drunken cowboy, had scrawled, "This means saloon," in the thick lead of a carpenter's pencil.

A handful of horses were hitched at the post on one end of the building, and a trough was set under the cross rail, a rusted pump at one end, its wooden handle splintered recently enough that the raw wood stood out against the weathered gray of the rest of it.

McMasters tied the roan, used a rusted coffee can full of water scooped from the trough to prime the pump, and jerked the handle several times until water gushed into the trough.

He took off his hat and leaned over to scoop water to his face and rinse off a little of the dust, then rinsed his mouth and finally swallowed a couple of gulps of the tepid water.

Then he spotted a couple of *vaqueros,* their sombreros resting on their backs, riding in the direction of the cantina, and watched them moved past before he pushed aside the spring-loaded butterfly doors and stepped into the shady interior. After the harsh sunlight, the gloom of the cantina blinded him for a few moments. He was aware that conversation had stopped. Then he heard someone say something about a gringo, and several men laughed. By then, his eyes had adjusted to the dim light, and he looked around.

Several tables were scattered around the single large room, most of them empty. He was the only Anglo in the place, and his Spanish was not great. But he knew how to order a beer, and he stepped to the bar, where a white-haired man with crinkled skin around his smiling eyes swiped at a pool of water on the gleaming wood.

"*Señor?*" the man said, tucking the rag into the waistband of his jeans under a swelling paunch. He looked at McMasters expectantly.

"*Cerveza, por favor.*"

"You sure you want a beer, *señor*? Mexican beer is, well . . ." He tilted his head as if in apology for the quality.

McMasters nodded. "A beer'll be fine."

"Okay, *señor.* It is your belly." He patted his midsection, chuckling, then added, "And I am the expert on bellies, as you can see."

McMasters grinned. "I never argue with an expert," he said.

The *cantinero* reached under the bar and pulled out a long-necked brown bottle. It sported a label with a name McMasters had never seen, "Rio del Oro." Prying off the lid, the *cantinero* asked, "You want a glass, *señor*?"

McMasters shook his head. He'd drunk out of worse than a bottle, but saw no need to share that with the roly-poly Mexican. The chubby man pushed the bottle across the bar. "You are a long way from home, *señor,* no?"

"I suppose I would be, if I had a home."

The barkeep shook his head sadly. "It is a bad thing to have no home, *señor.* I used to be like that, go where the work was, like a tumbleweed, roll against a fence and stick for a while, then the wind she would change, and I would roll away to some other place." He spread his arms wide. "Then one day I told myself it was better to live where the work was, and I made this place." He cocked a thumb over his shoulder toward a door in the corner. "Now I live in back and work in front. There is always work, as long as men are thirsty. And they are always thirsty, so I am always here."

McMasters took a sip of his beer before answering. "You're right about this beer, *señor.*"

The Mexican grinned. He started to say something, but stopped, suddenly staring over McMasters's shoulder.

Turning, McMasters saw two men getting up from a nearby table. The *cantinero* said something in Spanish that McMasters didn't catch, but the two men frowned at him, one raising a finger in a threatening manner.

Planting themselves directly in front of McMasters, one on either side of him, they folded their arms across their chests. Both wore sombreros and colorful shirts. One wore a conventional gunbelt, a pearl-handled Colt on his hip. The other had his holster on backward on his left hip, for a cross-draw, and had a bandolier over his shoulder, half of the leather loops empty. They looked enough alike to be brothers, or bookends.

The one on the left was slightly taller and slightly heavier. It was he who spoke.

"You don't like Mexican beer, gringo, I think maybe you should go back to Texas, no?"

"I don't see that it's any of your business, amigo," McMasters answered.

"I don't go to a gringo saloon and complain about gringo beer or gringo whiskey."

"Then you're a wise man, *señor*. But even wise men can make mistakes, and you are about to make a very bad one."

The man smiled broadly, looking at his companion for a moment, then, faster than a striking rattler, went for his gun. But McMasters was faster. He clamped the man's wrist in an iron grip, arresting the draw and then spinning the man around with a whip-cracking motion until he bounced off his companion. Letting go, McMasters drew his own gun, thumbing the hammer back in the same motion. It grew quiet.

"I came in here to have a beer," he said, nodding toward the bottle on the bar behind him. "I intend to do just that. Now, if you want to live to see that bottle empty, you go sit down like a good boy and mind your own business. *Comprende*?"

The man glared at him, but nodded. He started to turn, but McMasters stopped him. "Unh, unh, unh. Not so fast. Leave your guns on the bar."

The two *vaqueros* thumped their pistols on the bar, then went back to their table, grumbling. They finished their drinks and stood up to leave the cantina, and McMasters called to them. "You forgot your guns, amigos," he said. The *cantinero* looked at him in surprise, shaking his head that it was a bad idea. But McMasters insisted.

The *cantinero* handed him the pistols, and he opened each to remove the bullets, then walked over, handed the pistols to the two men, set the fistful of ammunition on the table, and said, "No hard feelings . . ."

The two men glared at him, snatched their pistols and crammed them into their holsters, then scooped up the bullets and backed toward the door, as if they expected McMasters to shoot them in the back. When they were gone, McMasters walked back to the bar and finished his beer, then ordered a second.

The *cantinero* gave him the beer, then leaned across the bar. "That was very foolish, *señor*. Those are very bad men."

"I'm a very bad man too, *señor*," McMasters said.

"No, you don't understand. They are very *bad*."

Curious, McMasters sipped his beer then leaned closer. "How bad? What are they, *banditos*?"

"Something like that, *señor*. I can't tell you now. Later, I will explain."

McMasters was intrigued. "All right. I'll come back later. What time do you close up?"

"Late, *señor*. Midnight."

"Can you tell me someplace in town where I can get a room?"

The man nodded, relaxing now that the conversation had moved onto ground he considered less perilous. "*Sí*, my brother runs a little boardinghouse down the street where you can get a room for the night. I wouldn't if I was you. If I was you, I would get on my horse and bid adios to Las Palomas. But you know best."

"That's right, *señor*, I do," McMasters assured him. "Where's the place?"

The *cantinero* pointed. "It is called Raul's Pension. One block. It's sign is *azul*, how you say, blue."

Eleven

McMasters was as good as his word. He walked into the cantina at midnight. It was all but deserted. The friendly *cantinero* was talking to two men, both of whom looked like farmers judging by their sandals, canvas pants, and the roughly woven ponchos thrown over their shoulders. The ponchos showed signs of once having been quite colorful, but the bands of red and blue were sunbleached, and years of wear had brought the beige fabric out in the faded remains of the stripes.

All three looked up when McMasters walked in, and the *campesinos* tossed off the rest of their tequilas and made excuses. They gave McMasters a wide berth as they headed for the door, watching him from the corners of their downcast eyes. They looked for all the world like men trying to bypass a serpent without drawing its attention.

When they were gone, the bartender gave McMasters a broad grin. "Did you sleep well, *señor*?"

McMasters nodded. "Raul's place was very comfortable. And cleaner than I had any right to expect."

"My brother is like me, *señor*. He thinks that if you do the right thing by your customers, they will do the right thing by you. We learned that in Los Estados Unidos, in New Mexico. We were born there, longer ago than I care to remember. Many Mexicanos don't like gringos. But to me, they are just pale people who wear funny hats.'' He laughed, a phlegmy rattle that made him sound like he was going to choke, then finished his own tequila. ''A drink, *señor*. On *la casa*?''

Before McMasters could answer, the man poured himself another tequila, then got a glass for his guest. After pouring the second drink, he went to the front, closed a heavy wooden inner door, and dropped a thick timber bar in place. Walking back to the bar, he said, ''Sometimes thirsty men get impatient. I learned a long time ago that a strong door is better than a firm no.''

McMasters took a seat at the bar while the *cantinero* moved around behind the bar and poked his head through the open doorway leading to the rear of the building. ''Blanca,'' he called, ''Time to work, *chiquita*!''

Then he grabbed a rag and started to wipe down the bar, turning up the kerosene lamps to make it easier to see. McMasters was about to ask a question when a striking young woman appeared in the doorway.

The *cantinero* saw the look of surprise on his lone customer's face, and turned. ''Blanca,'' he said, ''clean off the tables, okay, *dulzura*.'' Then he turned back to McMasters. ''My daughter, Blanca,'' he said. ''I could not run this place without her. She helps in the cantina during the day. Then she sleeps in the evenings. It is no life for a young girl, but around here, there is no life anyway. Not for someone like her. Not with those men around. And I say that not just because she is my daughter.''

''What men? Those men who were here this afternoon? Is that who you are talking about?''

''*Sí*, them and those like them. There are many of them,

señor. Like ants sometimes on a piece of bread on the ground. And sometimes you don't see them for days or weeks. Again like the ants. I suppose they are always around somewhere, but they only come out when it suits them."

"But who are they?"

"*Quien sabe?* Who knows? I only know there are many of them, and they are trouble. You saw those men who were here when you came in?"

McMasters nodded. "Farmers, weren't they?"

"*Sí,* farmers, yes. And they thought you were one of those men. That's why they left so quickly."

McMasters started to say something, but the *cantinero* raised a hand. "I know, you are going to say that it should be obvious, even to ignorant farmers, that you are a gringo. But these men I tell you about, they are gringos and Mexicanos both. But they are all alike."

"I don't see why it should have mattered to them, even if I was."

The bartender snorted derisively. "That is because you don't know what it is like to work all year to raise a little food for your family and a little more to sell to buy seed for the next year, so you can do it all over again. Then one day, when you bring in the little bit of corn you have been able to grow, these men come along and take it from you, say they need it for their horses, and they take it away and don't even leave a single peso behind to pay for what they have taken. If you are lucky, which being a *campesino* you already know you are not, you will get back your wagon and your mules."

"That happens here?"

"Oh, *sí,* that and more. There is a camp in a box canyon south of here where these men live when they are not off doing whatever it is they do."

"And what exactly," McMasters asked, leaning forward, "is it that they do?"

The *cantinero* shrugged. "I think they steal cows, *señor.* That is what I think. I have heard them talk when they come in here, and by the time their tongues are loose, they are very drunk, and it is hard to follow what they say because I have to pretend that I am not even listening. But I think they steal cows."

"For the meat, is that what you mean? They steal cows to feed themselves?" McMasters sensed that he was getting close to what he needed to know, but did not want to misunderstand what the *cantinero* was trying so obliquely to tell him. To come so far only to end up in a wild-goose chase would be infuriating.

The *cantinero* laughed, his phlegmy rattle filling the closed space and echoing from its four corners. "No, *señor,* not to eat. To *sell.* Sometimes they come in and they have a lot of money. Then they get very, very drunk, even more drunk than usual. They visit the *putas* in the whorehouses, and they even bring them here to get them drunk. Then, for many days or weeks, we don't see them. Sometimes, they stop here for a little taste of tequila and then they head for the border. Then later they come in again, all dusty and dirty, and that is when they have the money again. And that is when they get very drunk and show us just what they are like."

"And you think they steal the cows across the border, is that it?"

"Mostly, *sí.* Sometimes the rancheros here have trouble, but only some of them, and not very much trouble either. It is like a joke around here, *señor.*"

"What about the *federales*?"

The *cantinero* scowled. "What about them?"

"Why don't they do something about it? Why don't they just arrest these men?"

The *cantinero* wiped the bar more vigorously, but did not answer. McMasters was about to ask again when he heard footsteps approaching him from behind. He turned to see Blanca staring angrily at her father. Her dark eyes were flashing, and McMasters wondered whether it was just the lamplight or her anger that provided the sparks. She looked to be in her early twenties, except for her hands, which were work-hardened and looked to be those of an older woman. Her bosom, heaving with suppressed anger, was ample, the soft curves rising above the snug bodice of her flowered dress. But her face was smooth, the pouty lips dark pink, and the cascades of coal-black hair sparkled as if changing to diamonds before his eyes.

"Why don't you tell him, Papa? Why don't you tell him the *federales* take money from these men? Why don't you tell him that the *federales* take orders from the governor of Tamaulipas, who takes orders from the Presidente in Mexico City, and that both men line their pockets with money from these stolen cows."

"Hush up, Blanca," her father snapped. "There is no need to—"

"The man asked you a question, and you didn't answer it. You answered all the easy ones. You are like the others. You complain and you whine, but there is a line that you refuse to cross, and that is why those men will always be able to do what they do. Because no one cares enough to stop them. Especially not the governor or the *federales*. And you and the other people who live here are afraid of what will happen if they are driven away anyhow, because this is where they spend all their money. When they bother to pay for things they take, which is not often."

"Blanca!"

The *cantinero* was stern now, even angry, but Blanca was not cowed. She simply shook her head and then looked at

McMasters. "You have to excuse my father, *señor*. He is a good man, but he is frightened. All the people of Las Palomas are frightened, because they are not strong enough to protect themselves, and the *federales,* who are supposed to protect them, do nothing."

She turned away then, and went back to clear off another table and wipe it down with a damp cloth. McMasters watched her, the straight back, the proud shoulders, the way she tossed her black hair, still angry, the anger having nowhere to focus. She could not completely blame her father, but she included him in her indictment.

"Blanca," the old man shouted. "You should not discuss our business with strangers. Go in back. Now!"

She glared at her father for moment. Then, without a word, she stomped across the floor, slammed the damp cloth onto the bar, and disappeared into the back room.

"You must forgive her manners, *señor*. Sometimes, you know, she has a little too much fire in her belly. I guess it is being young. It is so long ago, I don't really remember. But her mother was like that too. That much I do remember." He smiled sadly, remembering her.

"She is just worried about you," McMasters said. "By the way, you never told me your name, *señor*."

The old man smiled and stuck a hand across the bar. "Pedro Morales y Sevilla. A proud name for such a foolish old man to carry, is it not?"

"You are not so foolish, *señor*. Just prudent. That is hardly foolish."

"Sometimes I wonder about the difference between prudence and cowardice, *señor* . . ." He waited for McMasters to supply his own name, and when he did, said, ". . . Boyd."

"It is a fine line, that is true," McMasters said. "But I think that if you have to cross it, then you'll know. And I think too that you will come down on the right side. Until then, I wouldn't worry about it.''

"Would you forgive a prudent old man an imprudent question, Señor Boyd?"

"It would be rude not to, I think," McMasters said, smiling, then taking another sip of the tequila. "What is your question?"

"You seem to have an uncommon interest in these bad men. Even an imprudent interest."

"But not foolish?"

Morales laughed. "No, not foolish. Or at least I do not think so."

"And I hope you are right."

"Your interest, *señor*?"

McMasters nodded, letting Morales know he was debating whether, and how, to answer the question. He sipped more tequila, feeling the burn as it slid down his gullet, knowing that he was getting close to his limit, and finally sighed. It might be risky to tell the old man anything, but he might never have a better opportunity to find out what he needed to know.

Finishing his tequila, he set the glass down with exaggerated care. He remembered the gesture from the misty past, the time of a perpetual drunken haze. Only this time he was not drunk, just preoccupied, and the habit had surfaced from somewhere deep inside him.

"I am interested in learning about these men," he said. "Very interested." He let the open-ended nature of that interest resonate in the sudden silence.

"You want to do something about these men, *señor*? Is that it?"

"Possibly. If they are the men I think they are, and steal their cows from the places I think they steal them, yes."

"That will get you killed very quickly, *señor*."

"I am willing to take that chance."

"Perhaps so. But perhaps you ought not to be."

"These men," McMasters said, "if they are who I think they are, steal many cattle in Texas, and they drive them across the border to sell. The men who rightfully own those cattle want this to stop. And they pay me to make it stop."

"By yourself, *señor*? Not possible."

"Not by myself, no. I will have help when the time comes. But first I have to make sure I understand what I am up against."

"Then you should go see for yourself. You should ride to the camp, see how many men there are. Then, if you still think this is something you want to do, you should go and get all the help you can get, because you will need it, *señor*. And that is not foolishness I am talking. It is the truth."

"Do you know where the camp is?"

"*Sí*. I know this. I have not seen it with my own eyes, you understand, but I know."

"Will you tell me?"

Morales shrugged. "I don't think that would be a good idea, *señor*. For me or for you."

"If you don't tell him, Papa, then I will."

Both men turned to see Blanca standing in the doorway, her hands on her hips, the angry blaze back in her eyes.

Morales sighed. "Do you have any children, *señor*?"

The question took McMasters by surprise. It stabbed him under the ribs as surely as a knife blade, and the pain must have crossed his face, because Morales reacted.

"I am sorry if I have asked something painful, *señor*."

McMasters waved off the apology. "It's all right."

Morales sighed again. "If you don't have children, *señor*, you cannot know how angry they can make you." He paused to look at Blanca for a moment. "Especially when they are right and you are wrong. I will tell you, because Blanca is right."

Twelve

It was noon, early for an honest thirst, but you couldn't prove it by the patrons of Pedro Morales's cantina. The place was packed, most of the customers drinking heavily, toying with the food that sat on the tables, shredded chicken congealing in its own grease, lettuce wilting in its taco shells. The place smelled of refried beans and saffron rice.

Pedro raced back and forth behind the bar, scurrying like a circus clown trying to put out a fire. Blanca and two other young women hurried to the tables with bottles of beer, glasses full of mescal and tequila, and the occasional *norteamericano* whiskey balanced precariously on wooden trays.

The women had to have nerves of steel to avoid the pinching fingers of the patrons, who were mostly Mexicans, with a sprinkling of gringos thrown in. McMasters stayed in one corner, trying to blend in with the background, but now and then he would catch one or another of the Mexicans giving him the eye, as if trying to place him, as if he was someone they had seen someplace before but didn't quite know where.

He was hoping that Carlito and the chubby Texan wouldn't put in an appearance, because there was no place to hide and he'd never make it out the door if he had to run.

The cantina got louder and louder as the men drank more and more. Scraps of conversation, mostly in Spanish too rapid for his rusty grasp of the language, fought with one another for attention. Once he heard the name Allison, or thought he did, and tried not to react. But he tried to pinpoint the table from which the name had come. Six men, all Mexicans, sat there, their heads lolling from their drink, their sombreros pushed off their heads and hanging down over the backs of their chairs.

Blanca brought him a drink, water with a slice of lime to disguise it as tequila. "Papa says you should at least look like the rest of them," she explained, leaning over to whisper in his ear, and resting a hand on his shoulder. Then she gave him a coquettish smile.

McMasters nursed it as if it were the genuine article, even once putting a little salt on his thumb and squeezing the lime juice into the salt before taking a sip. He grimaced at the taste, but managed to repeat it once before dropping the rest of the lime into his glass.

It was obvious that he was not going to learn anything on his own, and he hoped that Blanca and the other two women were keeping their ears open, as Pedro had instructed them to do. He was already certain that some of these men were the rustlers, but proving it would not be easy. He would have to catch them in possession of stolen cattle, and the only way to do that was to track them on a raid, or intercept them on the way back. In either case, he had to know where they intended to strike, and when. Only then could he gather Allison and his fellow ranchers and put together a large enough force to run them down. By himself, he would be reduced to sniping at long range, and a war of attrition was no solution. From the looks of things, whoever had organized the rustlers had more men than McMasters had bullets.

More important than catching them in the act was learning

the identity of the man or men who bankrolled them. He had considered the idea of lying in wait for a straggler, then trying to force the information out of him, but that was a long shot, and he didn't know enough yet to ask the right questions or to tell whether the man might be lying to him.

No, the best thing would be to track a stolen herd and follow it right to the front door of the rustlers' paymaster, then roll it all up in one bundle and put the operation down with a single blow.

The cantina was hotter than hell. He finally had to get outside, get away from the stink of beans and the even stronger smell of sweating, unwashed bodies that filled the cantina with its sour swelter. He had to weave his way among the crowded tables, and when he stepped into the blazing sun he felt as if he had just been let out of prison. The stink followed him outside, and he walked around to the side of the building, then around back. He stopped abruptly when he found two *vaqueros,* obviously drunk, each propped against the back wall with one rigid arm, pissing noisily against the base of the wall. McMasters mumbled an apology and backed away, but neither man paid any attention to him.

At the side of the cantina, he sat down in the shade, leaned back, and closed his eyes. He listened to the men muttering to themselves, but as near as he could tell, it was the usual boastful chatter about what they'd do to the serving women if only they got the chance. McMasters smiled to himself. He knew what Blanca thought of the drunken cowhands, knew the men's ears would be scalded if she ever decided to let loose with her opinions.

Then, to his surprise, he heard someone speaking English. Like the two Mexicans, the man was drunk. McMasters heard a new stream of water spewed against the wall of the building, and then the new man mumbled something he couldn't catch. But the new man wasn't finished. "Rosales'll have your *cojones* you screw this up," he added.

"Rosales don't scare me, *señor*," one of the Mexicans responded. "I pick him up and squeeze him like a fucking lime if I want to, till the juice run down his leg." He laughed, and the other Mexican chimed in.

"That juice is yellow, Ricardo. Like the lemon. Not lime juice, huh?"

Both of them laughed uproariously, but the gringo was not amused.

"Shut the hell up! You idiots better hear what I'm sayin' to you, because if you don't, and Rosales has to tell you himself, you'll be the sorriest pair of beaners ever drew breath."

"Don't you call me no beaner, you fuckin' gringo. I don't have to take that."

"You'll take it and like it, Ricardo. Now listen, we're leaving tomorrow morning. This is a big one, you understand? Rosales wants three, maybe four thousand head, and he wants 'em right quick. He's got a buyer all lined up, and there ain't much time. You understand me?"

"*Sí*, gringo, I understand. You think I am stupid. Four thousand cows. Quick. What is so difficult to understand about that?"

"You better get your ass inside and haul them drunken bastards out. I want to leave bright and early. Sunup, you hear me?"

"*Sí*, I hear you." Somebody belched, and then McMasters heard the telltale groan as a man bent over and spewed the contents of his stomach against the wall with a sickening splatter. *"Dios mio,"* the man groaned. "All that good tequila wasted. Now I have to go drink some more."

"You have another drink and I swear to Christ I'll put a hole in your gut. You hear me?"

"You are one nasty man, *Señor* Cartwright. Like a goddamned snake."

"You better believe that, Ricardo. You're drunker than any man has a right to be, and I won't have you drinkin' no more. Now go on inside and roust those assholes. I want them back at the camp in one hour. You hear that? Sixty minutes. *Una hora.* No later. Anybody comes in after that can kiss my ass and go find himself another job, because he's finished with me."

"I'll talk to Don Rosales."

"You can talk to any damn body you please. Rosales put me in charge, and I make the goddamned rules. Now git!!"

The two Mexicans grumbled, switching back to Spanish again, and McMasters heard their drunken footsteps move unsteadily away. Then a door banged. Then more steps, this time approaching, and McMasters tilted his hat forward and buried his chin in his chest. He saw the shadow of a man in a Stetson spill past the corner of the building. Then the rounded form of a potbellied man took shape on the sand as the man reached the corner and turned.

A pair of boots appeared at the edge of McMasters's field of vision, stopped for a moment, and then walked right up to him. He kept his eyes closed and snored once, letting his breath out in a shuddering rattle.

"Hey, cowboy," a gruff voice said. "You awake?"

The voice sounded vaguely familiar, but McMasters didn't dare look up.

"Cowboy, I asked you a question. You awake?"

McMasters kept his poise. One of the boots reached out, prodded him under the ribs, and he mumbled something, shifting his body the way he hoped a sleeping drunk would. The boot drew back, then poked him again, this time a little harder. He grunted, swiped at the boot with one hand, and turned away. The man seemed satisfied that McMasters was asleep, and hadn't overheard his conversation with the two Mexicans. He stepped over McMasters's outstretched legs, took a few steps, and then stopped again.

McMasters heard the rasp of a match, then smelled the sharp tang of tobacco burning. The match, still smoking, landed on his jeans, and he ignored it and the sharp pain that seared his thigh through the faded denim. Cartwright grunted, then walked off, his boots crunching on the sand.

Desperate to get a look at the owner of the familiar voice, McMasters rolled onto his side, cradled his head on one bent arm, and opened his eyes a crack. The man was twenty-five feet away, heading toward a general store across the street. But there was no mistaking the man's shape, and when he turned to glance back at McMasters one last time, the mustache confirmed the suspicion. It was the chubby Texan who had been with Carlito outside San Pedro.

Cartwright puffed thoughtfully on a little cigarillo, keeping it clamped firmly in his teeth and letting the smoke out through his nostrils in two tight streams. Removing the cigarillo for a moment, he spat a long amber stream into the dirt, swiped at it with the toe of one boot, then turned and continued on his way.

McMasters lay there for several minutes, wondering about the Rosales mentioned by Cartwright and the Mexicans. It was a common name in Mexico, but one of the vaqueros had said *Don* Rosales, and that narrowed the field considerably. There couldn't be more than a handful of men named Rosales in this part of Tamaulipas with that honorific. Could it be a coincidence? McMasters wondered. Ben Allison's wife was a Rosales, his brother-in-law ran Allison's ranch, and another brother-in-law was supposed to be governor of the Mexican state. McMasters sure as hell couldn't make any accusations, not on such slender evidence, but it just as surely bore looking into.

Cartwright had gone into the store by the time McMasters dared get to his feet. He quickly moved behind the cantina, out of sight of the general store, and walked along the rear of the cantina, avoiding the foam-flecked dampness at the base of the wall. He slipped inside an open door at the rear, and found himself in the living quarters.

Peeking into the front of the cantina, he saw the *vaqueros* finishing their drinks, two men who must have been Ricardo and his friend moving from table to table, whispering to the men and turning aside their whispered protests. He couldn't hear what was being said, but it was obvious the news came as both a surprise and an annyoance. The men were not happy, but they got slowly to their feet as their glasses emptied, and started to drift out into the street by twos and threes.

Ten minutes later, all but Ricardo and his friend had left the cantina, and McMasters could see Blanca and her two helpers starting to move among the tables, starting to clean up the mess. The two men dropped into a pair of chairs, and one of them snatched at one of the girls as she went by. The girl tried to tear loose from his grip, but the *vaquero* refused to let go.

"Bring us tequila, you *puta*," he demanded, pounding on the table with the flat of his hand.

The girl continued to try to free herself, but the *vaquero* grabbed a fistful of her hair and forced her to her knees. "You won't bring me nothing to drink, then maybe I got something for you to drink, huh, *puta*?"

He fumbled in his lap, but McMasters couln't see what was happening because his view was blocked by the girl's head and shoulders. Then Blanca moved in and slapped the *vaquero* across the face. He grunted, cursed, and let go of the girl, but he caught Blanca by the skirt as she tried to move away.

He got up and pinned her arms to her sides with a bear hug, then took a fistful of her hair and forced her to her knees. His fly was open, and it was apparent what he intended. Pedro, having heard the noise, came out from the kitchen, and suddenly appeared in McMasters's line of sight.

"Mind your business, old man," the *vaquero* said. "This *puta* is thirsty and I have something for her to drink."

Pedro started to move toward the *vaquero,* but the second cowboy drew his pistol and prodded the old *cantinero*'s belly with the muzzle of an old Colt .44, forcing him back.

The *vaquero* who held Blanca's hair started to force her head toward his groin and the stiffening member protruding from his fly. McMasters couldn't stand by and watch. Not something like this. He remembered only too well the taunts hurled at him by the Winslow gang, telling him what they had done to Hannah and what they had forced her to do to them. He felt his blood boil as he drew his Colt and stepped through the doorway into the cantina's barroom.

"That's enough, you pigs!"

The *vaquero* pressed Blanca's head in against his belly, and said, "You mind your own business, gringo, or maybe I give you a drink too, eh?"

That was all it took. Thumbing back the hammer, McMasters leveled the Colt. "Let her go or you're one dead *cochino*!"

The *vaquero* laughed, his open mouth revealing several nubby yellow teeth with more than a few gaps between them. McMasters showed his own teeth in an even smile. Then he squeezed the trigger. The *vaquero,* his mouth still open, but now in a surprised O, fell backward, his chest already covered with blood, and sat down heavily. Thumbing the hammer back once more, McMasters aimed the pistol at the remaining *vaquero*. "You have anything to say?" McMasters asked.

"No, *señor,* nothing."

"Good. Now, drop the gun and haul your ass out of here. Pronto!"

Thirteen

Pedro Morales shook his head sadly, looking at the bloody corpse sprawled on the floor of his cantina. "You should not have done this thing, *señor.*"

"It's not like he gave me any choice, Señor Morales," McMasters answered. "You saw what was happening. And his partner had his gun already drawn. I'm sorry if I caused you any trouble, but I didn't think there was anything else I could do."

"I am not worried about trouble for myself, Señor Boyd." Morales explained. "These men shoot each other all the time. They get drunk and they are spoiling for a fight, and if there isn't anyone else around, they fight with each other. But you are not one of them, *señor,* and for this they will be very angry. The one you let get away, he will bring the others, and they will look for you. They will hunt you down like a wild animal, and if they catch you alive, it will not be pleasant what they choose to do with you. Then you will wish you were dead."

"Don't worry about it, Señor Morales. I know I won't."

"But you should, Señor Boyd," Morales insisted. "Believe me, I know these men, what they are like, and—"

"Look, I'll handle it. Where exactly is their camp?"

"On the river, a few miles south from here, but . . ."

McMasters raised a hand to cut him off. "Forget about it. I know what I'm doing."

He walked out into the street, and saw that Cartwright was still in the general store, standing just inside the doorway, as if wondering what had happened at the cantina. But if he was worried, he didn't show it. It was more an idle curiosity that seemed to have brought him to peer into the street.

McMasters hurried from the cantina, heading for the livery stable at the other end of town. Morales might have been right about one thing. Shooting the *vaquero* might have stirred up some trouble, but as long as he kept his wits about him, he might be able to use it to his advantage.

More than anything else, he wanted a look at that camp, wanted to get a clear idea of what he and Allison were up against. And the only way to judge the lion was to size him up in his own lair, and that was exactly what McMasters planned on doing.

At the livery stable, he saddled the roan in a hurry, handed the stable keeper a few pesos, and swung up into the saddle. When he rode out into the street, he could see Cartwright two blocks away, crossing toward the cantina. At first, McMasters thought the Texan was going to go inside, but he turned the corner of the building and a moment later reappeared in the saddle of a big black stallion. His tack was dazzling, silver disks at every turn, all of them catching the sunlight and sparkling like the crown jewels of some tasteless empire.

Cartwright didn't bother to look up the street to where McMasters sat on the roan. Instead, he jerked the reins and headed south, out of town. The Texan had been drunk, probably still was, and that gave McMasters an edge. It shouldn't be too difficult to follow him without being seen. With any luck at all, Cartwright would lead him right where he wanted to go.

McMasters waited until the Texan was just a tiny figure past the far end of town, then spurred the roan and headed after him. As he passed the cantina, he saw Pedro Morales dragging the body of the dead *vaquero* out into the street, holding the corpse by the ankles. He might have been putting out trash for all the concern he showed.

Morales looked up, let go of one dead ankle, and raised a hand in farewell. *"Vaya con Dios, amigo,"* he shouted. "You will need Him to watch over you."

"I'll be back," McMasters called. He spotted Blanca just inside the open door of the cantina and waved, but she did not return the greeting. She stared at him as if he were a complete stranger instead of the man who had just intervened to spare her a humiliating brutality.

It didn't take long for him to get a comfortable distance behind Cartwright, who seemed in no hurry to get wherever he was going. He imagined the Texan had a monumental headache, and that his stomach was none too serene at the moment. Somewhere ahead of Cartwright, McMasters knew, was the *vaquero* he had chased away, probably riding hell-bent for the camp, either to spread the news or perhaps to rally his *compadres* for a mission of vengeance. But that would take a while, and as long as he was careful, Mc-Masters figured he could avoid running into a wolf pack of drunken *vaqueros* without much effort. More than likely, they would be wasting their ammunition, shooting into the air, cursing and kicking up enough dust to be seen for miles.

The camp was probably no more than a hour or so away. Morales had guessed the distance at a few miles. That, of course, was subjective, and depended on whether or not a man was anxious to get there. Cartwright was not, and that might mean two hours in the saddle, instead of one.

Now that he had time to think about it, McMasters realized that he'd been trying to place the face of the dead *vaquero*. The man had looked vaguely familiar somehow.
Putting him together with Cartwright suggested the possibility that it had been Carlito, but he didn't think so. But there
still was something familiar about the dead man. He'd seen
him before, he'd swear to it. But where?

It was nearly three o'clock by the time he saw the dust on
the southern horizon. So, he thought, the surviving *vaquero*
had rallied the troops. The terrain ahead was relatively flat,
but it was crisscrossed with a lacy network of rocky boulder-
strewn draws and dry washes, gouged in the stony soil by
the occasional heavy rains that rushed headlong into the Rio
San Juan for a few hours after each storm had passed, only
to sit, dry as dust, for weeks or months until the next storm
came along.

He still had some time before he encountered the outraged
avengers, but he was in alien territory, and figured he'd be
better off if he took cover at the first opportunity that pre-
sented itself. In the distance, just as he'd expected, he could
faintly hear the sporadic cracks of discharging pistols. Soon,
drunken curses would accompany the gunfire, until the whole
thundering herd rushed past, their rage well on the way to
being dissipated long before they reached Las Palomas.

More than likely, by the time they reached the little town,
most of them would have forgotten why they had come.
They would go into the cantina for a drink, then finally
someone would remember, and their anger would ignite all
over again. But McMasters would be long gone, and they
would end up riding back the way they'd come, no longer
angry but just a little drunker than before. Or so he hoped.

McMasters wanted to get a clear idea of the size of the

rustlers' band before he reported back to Ben Allison. But so far, he hadn't a clue. There had been more than thirty men in the cantina that morning. But Morales didn't know the total number of men in the camp. He knew there were others, men who were not in the cantina. At least, there had been other men with them at various times in the past. It could be, he'd said, that they had left the group, or that they had been killed or arrested. Or, McMasters knew, it could be that whoever gave the orders had a large pool of men on which to draw, perhaps twice as many as had been in the cantina. Maybe, McMasters thought, the number of men in the camp depended on the size of the herd they intended to steal.

He'd ridden another mile and a half before he came across a dry wash cutting across the trail. It had vertical sides everywhere except where the trail dipped to cross through it by heading down a forty-five degree slope on the north and up a similar slope on the south to get back to ground level. The two slopes looked as if they had been man-made, created with pick and shovel to make passage of the wash easier, probably to accommodate frequent traffic to and from Las Palomas and the rustlers' camp.

The sound of gunfire was louder but less frequent now, and under the sharp reports, McMasters could hear drunken singing, as several men tried to outdo one another in volume, if not musicality, bellowing at the top of their lungs, one voice rising to a crescendo, then stopping abruptly as the singer forgot the words, only to be picked up after a moment's hesitation by someone else.

McMasters pushed the roan away from the river. The trail was too close to the water, and there was virtually no cover between the depression in the trail and the river's edge.

The wash made a dogleg to the left, and he made the turn, rode another twenty or thirty yards, and dismounted.

From the saddle, he could see over the lip of the wash, and would have risked being seen by the passing mob. Once on the ground, he pulled the roan close to the southern wall of the wash, holding the big stallion by its bridle and pressing his back against the rocky sand of the wall.

He could feel some of the sand sift down into his collar as the drunken singing grew closer and closer. The gunshots were less frequent now, but so loud that he thought for a moment the men were heading right toward him. He held his breath, hoping he'd gone far enough off the trail and that the rustlers paid no attention to the hoofprints leading up the wash. The soil was soft and sandy and the roan's hooves had made deep impressions, but there had been no time to do anything to obliterate them.

The thunder of the approaching hooves seemed to make the ground tremble, but he thought that must be an illusion. There couldn't be that many men. Or could there? The frequent clink of an iron shoe on rock sounded like a miser counting his hoard, and then the thunder subsided as the mob slowed to negotiate the depression in the trail. He heard hooting and laughing as one of the men lost his seat and fell to the ground, then fired his gun in anger.

Christ Almighty, McMasters thought, please get a move on. Don't stop. Not here. Not now. He saw the first few men suddenly vault over the lip of the northern wall, one pulling off to the side and watching as the rest of the men negotiated the tricky passage. The man had his sombrero in his hand, and was waving it in a great circle as if trying to fan his *compadres* across the wash.

McMasters spotted Cartwright now, obviously still as drunk as the rest of them, his face looking red, even at that distance. He'd been wondering what had happened to the Texan, if he'd gone on back to the camp against the tide, or if he'd felt somehow compelled to ride as its master. The actuality seemed to be neither. Cartwright was going along, but in the middle of the pack. Just one of the boys, Mc-Masters thought.

The mob pushed on, the lone, sombrero-waving *vaquero* urging the last of his men up the slope to the northern side of the wash. Then even he turned and rode out of sight. Relieved of the need to pay attention to the tricky horsemanship required to negotiate the wash, the men started singing again, and once more gunfire punctuated the drunken revelry.

McMasters took a deep breath. Grabbing the reins, he tugged the roan back toward the slope, deciding to walk him back rather than ride, to stay hidden a little longer, making sure the rustlers had had enough time to make the next bend in the Rio San Juan before regaining the trail.

The roan's hooves clattered on the rocky litter that covered the floor of the wash. He turned the corner, expecting to see the silver glitter of the edge of the river. Instead, he saw the glint of sunlight on something else—the barrel of a Colt.

Planted there in the middle of the wash, legs spread wide, was the squat figure of a *vaquero*. In his left hand he held the reins to his horse, and in his right the Colt. The man seemed to waver, as if he were a mirage in superheated air, but when he thumbed back the hammer of the pistol, there was no mistaking the reality of the weapon in his stubby-fingered fist.

"I saw your hoofprints, amigo," he said. "The others, they were too drunk. But I saw them. I told them I had to take a piss, but I really wanted to have the pleasure of capturing you myself. It will be up to me what happens to you, and I have lots of interesting ideas." He laughed, showing one gleaming silver anomaly amid a mouthful of cracked, tobacco-stained teeth. Then, almost as an afterthought, he added, "You are the one who killed Ricardo. I saw you in the cantina."

"I don't know what you're talking about, amigo."

The man held the barrel of the Colt up as if it were an admonishing finger. "No, no, no, don't you lie to Pablo. I know it was you. I know this."

McMasters sorted through his options, but they were few. If he drew on the Mexican, the gunshot, whether his or Pablo's, might summon the mob back. If Pablo didn't get him, the mob would. But he was too far away to rush Pablo and try to overpower him. That left only biding his time, hoping Pablo would make a mistake. It was obvious the man wanted him alive, and would not shoot him unless provoked.

McMasters raised his hands over his head.

Pablo pointed to the gunbelt around his captive's waist. "You have to take off the *pistola, señor*. Unbuckle it and drop it on the ground."

McMasters reluctantly lowered his hands to his belt, opened the buckle, and let the gunbelt drop to the ground.

"Now, *señor*, back up a little."

McMasters did as he was told, and watched as the Mexican eased forward, waving the Colt in his chubby fist as if it were a magic wand. When he reached the gunbelt, he lifted it by hooking the toe of one boot under its middle. Letting go of the reins his fist, he retrieved the gunbelt from his upraised foot.

"This is a nice gun, *señor*," he said, his eyes flickering back and forth from McMasters to the customized revolver in the captured holster. Then something caught his eye, and he kept his eyes on the gunbelt. "These are funny bullets, *señor*. What are—"

But McMasters was on him, grabbing the man's gun hand and locking the Colt's hammer back with his own thumb to avoid an accidental discharge. The man let go of the gun as McMasters twisted it, bending Pablo's trigger finger, locked in the trigger guard, until it snapped like a matchstick. With a howl of pain, Pablo dropped the gunbelt and backed away, cupping the broken finger in his left hand for a moment, then shaking the injured hand rapidly, as if signaling to someone for help.

But he had all the help he needed at his waist. His left hand reached across his midsection and reappeared with a Bowie knife gleaming in its fist. He knew McMasters had the pistol, but must have known too that he dared not use it. "Why don't you shoot Pablo, *señor*?"

The Mexican laughed, then lunged with the Bowie held in front of him. McMasters could see by the grip that the man was no stranger to its use. He tried to grab the man's wrist, but the blade nicked him, and he backed up a step. Pablo followed, taking two shorter steps of his own. He was grinning.

"Going to gut you like a pig, amigo," he said. "Skin you, and fry it up like *tacos*."

Another step, then another, and suddenly McMasters was against the wall. Pablo darted forward, and McMasters lashed out with his foot as he fell to one side. He managed to trip the ungainly *vaquero*, who slammed into the wall right where McMasters had been standing a moment before. McMasters lashed out again with his foot as Pablo turned, catching him in the groin, and as he bent over, McMasters came up, grabbed the knife hand in both of his own, and twisted into Pablo's advance.

He heard the grunt as Pablo impaled himself on the eight-inch blade, then a sigh. Pablo groaned then, and a trickle of blood appeared at one corner of his mouth. McMasters gave the hand another push, and this time Pablo sank to his knees. McMasters let go, and Pablo folded his hands over the Bowie's hilt, looking as if he were about to pray. Then he tumbled forward, driving the knife even deeper into his gut. He shuddered once, arched his back like a landed trout, then groaned once more and lay still.

Fourteen

The camp was deserted. McMasters found several knocked-together shacks made of raw timber, and a few tents. The campfires were still smoking, and on one of them a pot of coffee hissed as the last of the water burbled out of the spout and boiled away, leaving a brown stain on the tarnished metal.

Walking around the campsite, he was reminded of stories he'd heard about the Civil War, how sometimes a unit would up and leave on the spur of the moment, and the other side would ride in and find the place quiet, as if everyone was in hiding for a surprise party, just waiting for the guest of honor to show his face.

He couldn't tell how many men lived here, but at least he now knew where it was. Climbing back on the roan, he rode the perimeter of the camp, then made a series of widening circles, trying to get the layout fixed firmly in his head. Located in a shallow, V-shaped valley, ending against high walls that ran together, it was well positioned for defense from the north, but its back, on the southern end, was another matter.

Pedro Morales had said it was a box canyon, but

McMasters wasn't so sure. Riding toward the wall that looked at first glance to be solid, he found that it actually became a steep-walled canyon nearly a quarter mile long. He rode all the way in, expecting to find that it ended in a blank wall, overlooked by the fifty-foot cliffs on either side. But the canyon suddenly broadened out again into another valley, leaving the back wide open. It looked almost as if the rustlers expected any opposition to come from the direction of Las Palomas, and probably not from the *federales,* who would probably know the terrain and that there was a back way into the camp.

McMasters rode back through the camp one more time, then opened his saddlebags for a notebook and a pencil, the roan restless beneath him as he sketched the layout and the canyon route for a rear assault. Satisfied that his sketch was accurate and that he had enough details, he dismounted and walked through the camp, peering into the shacks, poking his nose under the flaps of the tents. The shelters all smelled of sour bedding and sweaty clothes that lay in mounds in the corners. He found some books, mostly in Spanish, a few old newspapers, and an occasional weapon.

Defenseless at the moment, the camp almost begged him to ride through it with a torch, setting shacks and tents on fire, destroying bedding, foodstuffs, and the few boxes of ammunition he found in one of the shacks. But that would be a mistake. His best weapon was knowing more than the enemy. Set their camp on fire, and they might relocate. Even if they stayed put, they would know that their whereabouts were known, even if they had no idea by whom. No, it was better to head north, get Allison and his allies ready for the coming raid and, if necessary, a border crossing.

McMasters was still curious about the "Don Rosales" the *vaquero* had mentioned, and wanted to discover who he was before returning to Texas, even if that discovery might prove unpleasant for Allison and his family. But from here on out, McMasters knew he had to proceed on the assumption that there was a family connection and that his identity was known to the rustlers.

Instead of taking the river trail back to Las Palomas, he decided it would be safer to make a wide loop to the east and approach the town carefully. If the rustlers were still there, he'd head straight for the border. If they had vented their collective rage and gone back to their camp, he could ask Pedro Morales a few more questions before setting out for Texas.

He was still three miles from town when he saw the dust cloud heading south along the riverbank. He slowed as the roan climbed a gentle hill, and when he reached the crest, he dismounted, watching the roiling dust drift away on the breeze. The sun was beginning to drop lower in the sky. It was still more than an hour before sunset, but already the pall of dust was picking up a reddish-orange tint from the declining light. McMasters decided that it would be best to wait until sunset before reentering Las Palomas. Cartwright had seemed pretty determined to get all his men into camp that afternoon, and there was no reason to assume that he would be less concerned now, unless he left a couple of men behind to keep watch for McMasters.

Even in the early evening, the heat was intense, and McMasters grabbed his canteen to rinse his mouth and slake his thirst. He watched the dust recede as the sun went down. When he could no longer see the cloud, the sun was balanced on the horizon, its color changed from the yellowish white of high noon to a deep, almost bloody red.

Climbing back into the saddle, he headed for Las Palomas, covering the last two miles at a fast trot. At the edge of the town, he paused for a few moments, trying to get a feel for the place. It looked the same as when he had left that afternoon, but some sixth sense told him that things had changed. He kicked the roan and headed for Pedro's cantina.

A few horses and a few more mules lined the streets, hitched to the battered rails. The stink of their apples was heavy in the lingering heat, but McMasters was used to it. He considered stopping at the livery stable, but decided to hold off, against the chance that he might decide to head for the border that night.

At the cantina, he dismounted, tied off the roan, and walked to the front of the whitewashed building. It seemed strangely quiet. Not one other animal was tied to the hitching post, and not a sound came from the open windows of the cantina. When he reached the front door, he was surprised to find it closed. He knocked with his fist, and heard the dull drumming of his knuckles come back out through the open windows.

But there was no answer. He walked to the rear of the building, leaned into an open window of the living quarters, and called out, *"Señor* Morales, *que pasa?"*

But again there was no answer. He rapped on the back door, rattling the boards and making the latch creak and groan, but still no one answered. It was odd, but McMasters wasn't alarmed. Maybe Morales had just decided to pay someone a visit. With business likely to be slow that night, maybe it was a good time to catch up on socializing.

He walked back to the front and stood looking up the street, trying to make up his mind where to go next. There were two other cantinas in town, and he was hungry, so he started toward the center of town, built around a tiny plaza, with a church occupying the place of honor on the empty square. He walked across the plaza, suddenly aware that he had seen no one since his arrival. It was beginning to seem as if the town were deserted.

But as he reached the center of the square, he noticed that

the doors of the church were open. He stopped, heard the distant tinkle of a delicate bell, and realized that the sound was coming from the church. He walked across the plaza, mounted the broad steps, and reached the front door just as the congregation began to sing in a language he knew was not Spanish. He knew that Catholics used Latin in church, and assumed that was what he was hearing.

He took off his hat, and took a couple of tentative steps into the dim interior as the hymn swelled to fill the small building. The sweet smell of incense swirled around him. Suddenly the singing stopped, and he was embarrassed by the jingle of his spurs as he moved into the church.

He couldn't see clearly in the dim light from flickering candles, but he heard a sudden rustle as the parishioners turned in their pews to see who had come in so late. As his eyes adjusted to the gloom, he saw a rude box of raw timber sitting in the main aisle, down toward the altar. It took him a moment to realize it was a casket.

Immediately, he started searching the crowded church, looking for Blanca and Pedro. Neither one was visible, and he eased into an empty space in the rear pew while the priest waited impatiently for the disturbance to subside. As soon as McMasters had taken his seat, the parishioners turned back toward the front of the church, and the priest turned his back.

Once more, the soft tinkle of bells sounded, this time echoing in the enclosed space. The smell of the incense grew stronger, and the priest began to intone his prayers, the heavy cadence of the Latin sounding still more somber to McMasters now that he knew it was a funeral.

The parishioners answered the priest's prayers easily, the Latin words coming easily to their practiced tongues, despite the fact that most of them were unable to read, and only a handful referred to missals or prayer books open in their hands. When they knelt down with another rustle of cloth,

McMasters was embarrassed again, and an old woman next to him, already on her knees, reached back to grab him by the arm and pull him forward to his knees.

He tried to ignore the discomfort of the hard stone floor on his kneecaps, and hoped he would not have long to kneel. The priest was hurrying now, or seemed to be, as if he had some deadline that everyone in the church knew about except McMasters.

And then it was over. The priest came out from behind the altar rail, preceded by a pair of dusky young boys, their liturgical garments incongruous above their bare feet and the ragged ends of their canvas pants just peeking out from beneath the tiny cassocks.

The priest paused at the head of the casket and ducked down for a moment, and when he rose again, he held aloft a silver censer, gleaming in the candlelight. He shook it back and forth, the heavy silver cracking against thick silver links of chain from which it was suspended and which the priest held bunched in his fist. The censer smoked, and the priest waved it back and forth over the casket several times, then moved past the casket, leading the way as pallbearers moved to take the weight of the coffin on their shoulders. The priest held the censer high and waved it from side to side, filling the aisle with the fragrant smoke as the casket followed him toward the yawning front doors of the church and the pitch-black night beyond them.

As the priest passed, he gave McMasters a scowl, then looked away, and McMasters eagerly searched the faces of the pallbearers. But there was still no sign of Pedro or Blanca. Not until the casket passed did he spot the girl, her arms draped around the shoulders of an old man who finally looked up as he passed the last pew. With a sigh of relief McMasters nodded his commiseration to Pedro Morales. He was relieved the *cantinero* was safe, but who then was in the casket?

And what had happened?

The crowd filled the aisles, and McMasters was too much the outsider to leave his seat until the church was almost empty. Then he rushed out into the hot night and fell in behind the procession, which turned the corner of the church at the north end of the plaza and snaked its way alongside the church. The cemetery was out back, and several torches were blazing, staked in the mound of fresh earth, its moisture half gone, leaving it only a little darker than the dry ground on which it had been piled.

The pallbearers moved along either side of the open grave. Then, on a signal from the priest, they dropped to their knees, the casket rocking in their straining arms. Once they had found their positions on the ground, they looked to the priest for another signal, and when he nodded, they leaned forward, lowering the rude timber box into the hole until it thumped against the bottom. Several clumps of dirt fell from the lips of the grave walls, thudding hollowly on the wooden lid. The pallbearers got to their feet then, backing away from the grave, and Pedro and Blanca moved in next to the priest, who spread his hands over the open grave and intoned yet another prayer in Latin.

Blanca held a bouquet in her arms, and she knelt to reach into the grave and place it on the top of the casket. Pedro reached down to the ground, took a handful of earth, and held it in curled fingers out over the grave, letting it pour out in a stream that hissed as it rained on top of the coffin. A couple of pebbles clattered in last as he spread his hands wide, then clapped his palms together once to rid them of the last vestiges of earth. There was something altogether too final about the hollow thud of the small stones on the raw wood.

The parishioners filed past Pedro and Blanca, each stopping for a moment to offer condolences, some leaning over to kiss Blanca on the cheek, some clapping the old man on the shoulder and leaning close to whisper in his ear.

The priest was the last one to pay his respects, and when Pedro moved off, he stayed behind, directing two men to come out of the shadows and start to fill the grave. Even before Pedro reached the low fence around the cemetery, the rasp of shovel blades and the thumping of earth on the hollow box filled the night air.

Outside the cemetery, Pedro stopped, turned, and waited for McMasters.

"What happened?" the American asked.

"My brother, Raul. You met him, I think?"

McMasters nodded. "Yes, of course. The man who owns the boardinghouse."

Pedro nodded sadly. "He did, yes. Today, after you left, those men came back. They were looking for trouble and, I think, for you. When they could not find you, they settled for trouble, which is usually enough for them in any case. They were in the cantina, and they were making trouble. Raul tried to stop them from bothering Blanca and the other girls, but they were drunker than usual, and they were spoiling for a fight. One of them, a man they call Carlito, pulled his knife, and he stabbed Raul in the chest. I think the blade pierced his heart. He died in my arms, *señor*. My younger brother, he died in my arms." The old man started to sob, and McMasters reached out for him, but Blanca brushed his hands away.

"Leave him alone. Haven't you done enough, *Señor* Boyd?"

But Pedro reached out his own hands and took both of McMasters's hands. "It is not his fault, Blanca," he said, scolding his daughter in the gentlest of tones. "You said yourself that someone had to stop those men. That it was time we stood up to them. *Señor* Boyd stood up to them and spared you great pain. That is what he did, and in my eyes that was not a wrong thing. It is those men who are to blame, not *Señor* Boyd.''

Blanca did not agree, to judge by the anger in her beautiful face. She turned her back, and hugged her arms close to her chest despite the heat. Pedro patted her shoulder, then turned back to McMasters.

''Did you find the camp?''

McMasters nodded. ''Yes. It was deserted. I saw them coming toward Las Palomas, and gave them a wide berth, then went to the camp.''

''They are going north of the border tomorrow or the next day, *señor*,'' Pedro said. ''I heard them talking, especially that fat one, the one they call Cartwright. They are planning to steal many cattle, *señor,* many more than ever before.''

''There is only one more thing I want to ask you, señor Morales.''

''Ask it.''

''This governor Blanca mentioned the other day. What is his name?''

''Don Juan Rosales, *señor*. He is the governor of Tamaulipas. That is why they are able to get away with so much. But this time, I think, Don Rosales goes too far.''

''Does Rosales have family in Texas?''

''*Sí*, a brother and a sister. His sister is married to a powerful man, a Ranger they say, named Aleman, or something like that.''

''Allison. Ben Allison.''

''*Sí*, that is it.''

''Thank you, Pedro. You've been a big help. And I promise you that the man who killed your brother will not get away with it. I know who he is, and I will make him pay.

If I do nothing else, I will make him pay. I swear it.''

"You should be careful of making such promises, Señor Boyd. Sometimes a man means well, but . . .''

"I don't mean well this time, Pedro," McMasters said, staring toward the sky. "Not for Carlito. Not at all.''

Fifteen

McMasters left Las Palomas at nine at night. It was nearly four in the morning by the time he entered the town limits of San Pedro. Rather than call attention to himself by returning to the hotel, even though he had kept his room, he decided to find someplace out of the way where he could hole up until dawn. The only place that seemed likely was the former cantina where Margarita and Guadalupe lived.

He rode around the edge of town, approaching the old adobe building carefully from the town limits. There were no horses hitched at the old cantina, and there was no light in the window. He dismounted and walked the roan the last fifty yards, tied it to the rail, and rapped softly on the door. At first, there was no answer. He leaned in the open window and whispered, "Margarita? Guadalupe?"

If either woman was there, she must not have heard him, because there was no answer. Once more, he leaned in to whisper their names. And this time he got a response, but it was not what he was expecting. He felt the muzzle pressed against his temple, knew what it was, and froze.

He heard a door open, then felt another gun jammed into the small of his back.

"What do you want, *señor*?"

It was a woman's voice, another surprise. He started to turn, but the gun rapped against his spine, and he stopped, slowly raising his hands.

The gun moved away from his temple, and the woman behind him prodded him toward the front door. As he was forced inside, a match flared and the wick guttered for a moment before taking hold.

"Dios Mio," someone said. As his eyes adjusted, he saw Guadalupe, a pistol in one hand, the shaded lamp chimney in the other. "Oh, my God, *Señor* McMasters. I am so sorry," she said.

"Can I put my hands down now?"

Margarita answered from behind him. "Of course. We didn't know it was you. We were afraid, and . . ."

"It's all right, ladies. it's all right. I just needed a place to stay for the night, and I thought . . ."

"You thought you would come and have Guadalupe keep her promise, eh, *señor*?" Guadalupe smiled seductively. Her face was still bruised, but much of the swelling had gone down. It was now possible to see just how pretty she was. Dressed just in a silky chemise that took a pink hue from the tinted lamp, her more than ample figure was clearly outlined by the clinging cloth. Firm breasts, their erect nipples prominent against the soft silk, their aureoles like shadows on the silk, made him more than a little horny, even after the long ride.

He turned around to discover Margarita dressed in the same sort of filmy cloth. Her figure was less full, but no less appealing. Younger than Guadalupe, and leaner, she possessed an athletic grace as she crossed the room, her long legs pulling the cloth tight against her thighs and derriere as she walked to a table and set down the pistol.

"Maybe we should put out the light," Guadalupe suggested.

"That's a good idea," McMasters agreed.

Guadalupe lifted the chimney of the lamp, bent over, and paused long enough to give him a good look down the front of her nightgown. He noticed, and she smiled, then pursed her lips to blow him a kiss before extinguishing the flickering flame.

One of the women, he wasn't sure which, went to the door and locked it. He smelled her perfume as she glided by him in the darkness, and he tried to guess which of them she was.

In a husky voice, the woman said, "We have much to tell you, *Señor* McMasters. But first we have more important things to do."

On her way back, she stopped at his side, took him by the arm, and tugged him toward the back of the room where, he knew, the beds were. Hands worked at his gunbelt, and he quickly realized there were more than two. The gunbelt came away, then the busy fingers started on the buttons of his shirt and his fly. Peeling off his shirt, the hands fluttered over his chest and back, their touch delicate as the wings of butterflies.

Lips caressed his cheek, then dropped lower, tickled his chest, found a nipple, and sucked it gently until teeth nipped it once, then again. His jeans were tugged down around his ankles, then a firm push toppled him backward onto the bed. Immediately he felt his boots grasped firmly and jerked free. Then his jeans were removed and tossed aside. He heard them land against the opposite wall with a series of dull thuds.

"Ladies, ladies," McMasters said. "Wait, I have some important things to . . ."

But they ignored him, one of the women stopping his protest with a wet kiss. In the darkness he couldn't see who was who. He only knew that he was hungry for a woman, and since they seemed to be just as hungry as he, his questions would have to wait. He opened his mouth, letting the woman slide her tongue in, and returned the favor. Whoever it was sucked greedily on his tongue, and he felt hands stroking him, his chest, his thighs, his arms—they seemed to be everywhere at once.

He was already hard, but when a hand closed over him, he grew harder still. As the fingers begin to stroke him, another hand cupped his balls, squeezing gently. The woman atop him shifted her position, straddling him now, her hands braced on the bed on either side of his head. Poised over him, her legs wide, she lowered herself slowly while the disembodied hands held him rigid, guiding him toward the center of her. The head of his rigid erection was gently positioned, and he felt the tickle of a damp bush, then the fleshy wetness of thick lips as her heat enveloped him with a single downward thrust of her hips.

He groaned, and she leaned back, tossing her hair back until it brushed his thighs. Then she rose up slowly, until he thought he would be set loose again, but at the very height she stopped, then slowly lowered herself again, the slickness making a sucking sound as he was buried in her once more. She ground her hips, turning from side to side, rising slowly, then descending more slowly still. Her head was still thrown back, and he rested his hands on her hips for a long moment, trying to guess—Margarita, Guadalupe, he didn't know. And at the moment it didn't really matter.

His hands slid along her rib cage and as she rose again, her breasts eluded his greedy hands until she reversed her motion, lowering herself down to his hips again, her breasts moving into his waiting hands. They were full, the soft heaviness of them, the hardness of the nipples no clue to her identity. He knew only that she was moving faster now. Her skin was glazed with sweat, and her perfume mingled with the sharp tang of musk as she worked him harder and harder.

She was moaning now, her voice husky, an animal sound coming from deep in her throat that disguised it. He squeezed the full breasts gently, his thumbs working against the stiff resistance of her nipples. Rising and falling, now rapid, now impossibly slow, she teased him again and again to the edge of that explosion which he knew could not be denied but which seemed to be suspended now somewhere just beyond his reach.

He traced the curve of her throat with his trembling fingers, felt the hollows beneath her chin, the rigid bows of her collarbones, then grabbed her by the hips and held on as she started to move faster still. He was rising to meet her now, eager for release, but she withheld it, taking control and keeping it. He felt the ripple of her muscles against him as she withdrew, felt their hungry clutch as she returned.

Then a breast, not hers, appeared before him, and he opened his mouth to take it in. Full, full as the others, and still he had no idea whose as he sucked like a hungry child, tasting the saltiness of sweat, his tongue fluttering against the pebbled aureole. The breast was taken away, and he felt almost angry until its twin took its place, and again he tried to satisfy the nameless hunger in his gut.

It grew darker and he found his head clamped between damp thighs as the other woman straddled him, lowering herself, and his tongue found the damp jungle between her thighs, tasted drop after drop suspended there in the trembling tangle. He probed deeper, his lips brushing darker, thicker lips, his tongue sliding between them, tracing them, tasting their musky flesh, then sliding in still deeper, fluttering, looking for the hard center of her, finding it, and teasing her now, clamping gently with his teeth as she swiveled her hips and moaned in her own husky voice.

He stroked her back, brought his hands down to enfold the firmness of her ass, to feel the steady throb of her muscular thighs as she worked with him, following his tongue wherever it led her. Reaching around her broad back, he found her breasts, cupped them, tried to remember whether the first were larger—Guadalupe or Margarita, who was who?

He was moaning now as the women cried out, and their mingled scents swirled in a hurricane around him. The bed creaked beneath them, threatening to collapse under the weight of their passion, the violence of their motion, but he did not want to stop, could not even if he wanted. He was taunted by twin sirens, pushed higher and higher, until he thought he could see himself as if from a mountain, miles below, spread out beneath them, the tangle of limbs and trembling flesh one indistinguishable being as he merged with them so totally he thought he would lose himself forever in the fevered flesh they had all become, melting, surrendering their identities in pursuit of only one thing.

And then, the moment he thought would never come came rushing at him like a hawk dropping from the sky. He trembled, once, twice, then, urged on by the clamp of sweaty thighs at waist and mouth, he let go completely, feeling himself quiver and shake, and he thought that this moment too would never end. The woman impaled at his waist trembled and her throaty moan became a shriek, her body shaking as she joined him, and the woman above his greedy tongue gave her hips one last quivering thrust, grinding herself against him and raking her nails across his belly as she dug her hands into him and began to growl like a catamount, her fists beating against him then, the painless violence of her surrender hammering and hammering until she was drained and she collapsed on the bed beside him, her identity still a mystery.

He lay there, surrounded by the musk and the sweating

flesh, drenched in their juices and his own, his eyes closed, his strength sapped. He felt them leave him then, one at a time, the bed groaning once more as they got up. There was a whispered conversation deep in the shadows, but he was too exhausted to pay any attention to it. Even the giggling failed to tantalize him. He draped a trembling forearm across his face and tried to sleep.

They were back now, whispering to each other, one crawling onto the bed, the other kneeling beside it. He started to get up, but strong hands pressed him back against the mattress. A moment later, he felt the soothing caress of a damp cloth wiping away the sweat and cooling his fevered skin. Then another, as they washed him from head to foot, playful fingers teasing his wilted member back to attention as the cloth dabbed at his thighs and mopped the sticky residue from his stomach and hips.

His face too came in for their attention, the musk wiped away from his lips and chin, the sweat from his neck and chest. He felt so sleepy, so helpless, and half wondered if this was what it was like to be a baby about to be wrapped in swaddling clothes, or a corpse in its shroud.

At the moment, he didn't care which. He knew only that he belonged somewhere else, his tired brain and lifeless body longing to drift away. Once more, he closed his eyes and started to float off.

But as he was drifting off once more, he felt the bed sag again, and the women crawled in beside him, one on either side, their breasts pressed against his rib cage, their arms around his neck, their lips against his ears.

"We have to switch places, *Señor* Boyd," one whispered. And the other added, "Fair is fair, after all."

McMasters groaned, half in surrender and half in hungry anticipation. "Not now, ladies," he said. Please, not yet."

"All right," one whispered. "But soon, before the sun

comes up and it is too hot in here.''

''It's already too hot in here,'' he whispered.

They laughed, and as he drifted off to sleep, he felt their hands exploring him, every muscle in his aching, exhausted body caressed with gentle fingertips.

He tried hard to remember why he had come here in the first place, what had been so important that he had had to ride all night, but his body refused to let him concentrate on so mundane a matter. It told him that Cartwright and Rosales could wait. They would have to. He was too tired to do anything about them at the moment. And the thought of a rematch with the women was far too appealing.

Sixteen

Morning came and found McMasters staring at the ceiling. The women were already up and dressed, bustling around the stove. The smell of eggs frying caught his attention, and he realized just how hungry he was.

He sat up, the rustling pallet drawing Guadalupe's attention. She gave him a dazzling smile. "So, *Señor* Boyd, are we even?" she asked.

McMasters groaned. "Yes, we're even."

"Guadalupe always pays her debts, *señor*." She laughed, and McMasters could only shake his head. "But there is more. We have some information for you too."

Now he snapped alert. "What kind of information?"

"Those men you were wondering about. You wanted me to listen, and I listened. I know something that you don't know."

"What?" Anxious, he almost snapped at her, and she frowned her disapproval of his manners.

"After breakfast, *Señor* Boyd."

A table was already set, covered with a white cloth, three place settings arranged neatly. The utensils were mismatched, but everything was neat and clean, and McMasters marveled at the strength of character it must take to fight so hard to preserve some sense of normalcy for these women. He thought of his own slide into despair, how readily he had taken it, and he felt embarrassed.

He dressed quickly, ignoring the teasing of Guadalupe about his nakedness. Margarita was more reserved, but she observed him shyly, never quite looking at him directly but never quite taking her eyes off him either, until he buttoned his jeans and sat down to pull on his boots.

Guadalupe walked to the bed, took him by the hand, and tugged him toward the table, holding his chair until he took his place, then bumping it against the back of his knees until they buckled. When he was seated, she leaned over and kissed the top of his head. "We are like a little family, *Señor* Boyd, no? Maybe you would like to live with us?"

He wasn't sure she was teasing, and he looked up sharply. There was no way to tell from her expression whether she was serious or not. "I don't think so," he said. "I'm not much of a homebody."

"Too bad, *Señor* Boyd. Too bad."

Margarita sat to his right and Guadalupe served. After pouring coffee to go with the bacon and eggs, she took the chair on his left.

He ate greedily, while the women, far more dainty, took their time, sipping their coffee and cutting their food into tiny portions they ate with exaggerated gentility, dabbing with napkins at their mouths after every bite. Finally, the breakfast was finished, and after pouring more coffee, Guadalupe gathered the dishes and set them aside, then resumed her seat.

"There is a big raid coming, *Señor* Boyd," she said. "Many men are coming from Mexico to steal cattle, more than ever before."

McMasters did not reveal that this was not news. "How do you know?" he asked.

"I have heard it from three different men. Margarita has heard the same thing in the hotel where she works." Guadalupe looked at her for confirmation, provoking an energetic nod. "And they are coming soon."

"When?"

"One day. Two days. No more than that."

"You're sure about this?"

It was Guadalupe's turn to nod. "And I know who they work for. One of the men told me they work for a man named Don Rosales, and that he is a very powerful man in Mexico. This is why they are not afraid. They say he will protect them."

"Rosales?"

Again Guadalupe nodded. "*Sí, Señor* Boyd. I do not know his first name, but he is very rich and very powerful."

"Where will they take the cattle once they have them?"

"To Mexico. They will meet this man Rosales for their pay, and then he will take the cows to sell them in Matamoros."

"Do you know where he plans to meet them?"

Guadalupe moistened her lips. She seemed uncertain whether to share this part of the story with McMasters, but he pressed her. "Do you?"

Again, she nodded. "*Sí.* They have a camp in Tamaulipas. They will take the cattle there, where he will meet them with some *federales.*"

"How many *federales*?"

"Not many, I think."

McMasters sipped the rest of his coffee and got to his feet. "Thank you, Guadalupe," he said. He leaned over to kiss the top of her head, but she turned to look up at him. She stuck out her tongue and wiggled it with exaggerated lasciviousness. He returned the gesture, feeling a stirring he could not afford to act on as she sucked greedily on his tongue.

"Now you owe Guadalupe," she said.

"I too always pay my debts," he said, laughing. He glanced at Margarita, who seemed distant now, and when he kissed her forehead, she did not move.

He was ready to go, but stopped in the doorway, buckling on his gunbelt. "Guadalupe, don't tell anyone else about this, and don't tell anyone that I know."

"Don't worry, *Señor* Boyd. I want to collect what is owed me." Laughing, she blew him a kiss.

Hurriedly, he saddled the roan. He had to get to Ben Allison, and quickly. But he had to get the old Ranger away from Miguel Rosales to deliver the news that he knew was not going to be welcome.

All the way out to the Rocking A he tried to find a palatable way to present the information he'd gathered, and his suspicions based on that information. But no matter how he tried to soften it, it came down to one thing. One of Ben Allison's brothers-in-law, with the possible collusion of the other, was apparently behind the rustling, bankrolling the raiders, directing them, and giving them a safe haven in Tamaulipas, with the assistance of the *federales*. And there wasn't enough sugar in New Orleans to sweeten that bitter medicine.

By the time the hacienda came into view, McMasters was resigned to being the bearer of bad news, and he knew only too well what often happened to such messengers. But he had two choices. He could act on what he had learned, or he could ride back the way he'd come, go back to headquarters, and tell Warren that he had failed. Neither choice was pleasant, but only one involved a lie, and that made up his mind. He would tell Allison the news and let the chips fall where they may.

When he rode up to the house, Carmen and Rosalita were in the garden, both wearing jeans and denim shirts, sleeves rolled to the elbows, dirt smeared on sweaty forearms, as they ripped at weeds and planted flowers. They looked enough alike to be sisters, not quite twins, but not that far apart in age either. Ben Allison was in a rocking chair on the veranda, his benevolent smile broadening to a grin when McMasters dismounted and walked toward him, spurs jingling.

"Well, old son," the genial rancher said, "what did you find out?"

"We have to talk, Ben, and I mean now."

Allison patted an empty chair beside him. "Take a load off and let me hear," he said.

McMasters shook his head. "Not here. I want to talk somewhere private."

"Hell, ain't no place more private than a man's own home, is there?"

McMasters hesitated for a moment, then said, "Yeah, Ben. There is."

Allison scowled, then got to his feet with an exasperated sigh. "I'm gettin' too old for this shit," he said. "Supposed to be gettin' ready to ride off into the sunset in a pine box." He laughed, but it was halfhearted, and McMasters made no attempt to lighten the moment.

Allison walked off the verandah and into the garden, where he stood over Carmen and his daughter, watching them work for a few moments. Then he announced, "Me and Boyd got some business to attend to, Carmen. Be back in a little while, all right?"

Carmen Allison turned to look at McMasters, her eyes lingering for a long moment before finally engaging her husband's gaze. "All right, Ben. But you be home for dinner. Don't get so busy you forget about it, you hear?"

Allison nodded meekly. "I hear you."

Rosalita started to ask a question, but Ben shook his head. "Not now, honey, all right? I'll be back in a while. I'll tell you all about it then."

McMasters walked to the roan, and Allison mounted his own big gray, and said, "I guess we ought to go out to get Mike before we talk."

"No," McMasters said, more sharply than he'd intended. "That's not necessary."

Allison gave him a strange look, but nodded his acquiescence. "Whatever you say, Boyd."

McMasters led the way down the lane and out through the gate. Instead of heading onto the open range, he followed the road toward San Pedro for a mile or two, then moved out into the rolling grassland, heading for a stand of cottonwoods along a creek bank. Not until he'd reached the trees did he say anything, and then it was only to suggest, "This looks like as good a place as any."

Dismounting, he tethered the roan to some brush and walked down to the water's edge, where he squatted down to scoop up some water to rinse his mouth, then take a drink. Allison dismounted, hobbled his horse, and waited impatiently. When McMasters straightened up, the big rancher said, "All right, now what's the big secret?"

"You're not going to like it, Ben."

"Hell, there's lot's of things I don't like. I don't like mosquitoes and I don't like poison ivy. Don't care much for preachers, and I don't like bankers one damn bit. Lawyers are worse yet. So how bad can it be, whatever the hell *it* might be?"

Quickly, without sugarcoating, McMasters laid it all out, watching Allison's face as he spoke, the play of emotion-making the tangle of muscles along his jaw squirm like snakes. Pain darkened his eyes every so often. But Allison was patient, making no attempt to interrupt, hearing him out until the bitter end. Only then did he respond.

"You expect me to believe that bullshit, do you, Boyd?"

McMasters sighed.

"You expect me to believe that my own family is trying to ruin me, ruin the ranchers around here? My own family?"

"With all due respect, Ben, it's your wife's family we're talking about, not yours."

"Same damn thing, by God. Don't you split hairs with me, McMasters."

"I'm not splitting hairs, Ben. And I'm not expecting you to believe or disbelieve anything. All I'm doing is telling you what I've been able to piece together."

"But you believe it?" Allison studied him, looking for a hint of doubt, of malice. There was neither. "Don't you?" he asked again.

"I think so, yeah."

"Think so? That ain't good enough. Do you *believe* it, in here?" He rapped a big fist against his barrel chest, the sound like that of a bass drum.

McMasters thought it over, trying to frame his answer carefully but honestly. "It makes sense in a funny way," he said.

"How in hell does it make sense?"

"People on this end have all the information they need. It's no wonder the rustlers were able to strike when nobody was expecting them, get in and get out so quickly, and disappear. They knew where to go and when. With help on the other end, it was an easy thing for them to pull off. They don't have to find a market. They don't have to doctor the brands. They don't to have to worry about the authorities. All they have to do is run the beeves across the river, and they're home free. Juan Rosales takes it from there. A respected man, a powerful man, a rich man, who's going to argue with him, who's going to call him a liar when he drives the stock to Matamoros?''

Allison shook his head. "I don't believe you. You're a lying bastard, McMasters. And I'll tell you another thing. You're no kin to Warren McMasters, that's for goddamn sure.''

But McMasters stood his ground. "No, I'm not a liar, Ben, and you know it. I might be wrong, but I'm not lying.''

"You expect me to take the word of a bunch of whores and drunks against my own family?''

"I expect you at least to consider the possibility that it might be true.''

Again Allison shook his head. "No. I can't believe it. I won't believe it.''

"Ben,'' McMasters said, stepping closer and clapping a hand on the old Ranger's shoulder, "you don't have any choice. If there is one chance in a thousand that it's true, you have to find out. It's not just your stock and your ranch that are in jeopardy. Your neighbors are victims too. You owe it to them. You'd expect them to do what has to be done. You can't do any less.''

"Suppose you're wrong.''

"If I'm wrong, I'll apologize. If you don't tell your family, you and I will be the only ones who know. You don't have to tell the ranchers everything, just enough to get them to cooperate.''

"You are wrong, you know.''

"I hope so, but I don't think so.''

"So what do you want to do?''

"There's the rub,'' McMasters said. He took out a pack of Primeros, lit one, and tucked the box back into his pocket. "Here's how I think we have to handle it.''

Seventeen

All the way back to town McMasters debated with himself, sometimes even whispering aloud, trying to twist the possibilities into some shape that made sense, that was manageable, and most of all, that had a prayer of working.

He hadn't liked telling Ben Allison the news, hadn't liked seeing the disbelief in the old Ranger's face, hadn't liked when that disbelief turned to pain, as if every sentence were a knife blade slipped between his ribs searching for the heart. But it was true, and there was nothing he could do about it.

Ben Allison was resentful, and that was understandable. But he was also a pragmatic man. He knew that people sometimes do things that no one else can understand. And when those people are close to you, it is sometimes harder, not easier, to understand their motives. In the end, Allison had agreed to the plan, as much out of determination to prove McMasters wrong as because he thought him right. But Ben's motives were less important right now than his cooperation.

By the time he reached San Pedro, McMasters was no more comfortable with the situation. He had, instead, come to a kind of resignation, a recognition that events were now moving too fast for anyone to stop them. The only chance was to try to control them. But he was far from certain that was possible. He was like a kid on a runaway horse—all he could do was hang on for dear life and hope the horse got tired before he fell off.

He thought about staying with the women for another night, but worried that it would expose them to unnecessary risk, and finally decided against it. Instead, he stopped at the livery stable and put up the roan, then walked down the street, saddlebags draped over his shoulder, the big .70, its telescopic sight now attached, in his left hand.

When he walked into the hotel lobby, the clerk seemed surprised to see him. "Thought you were gone for good," he said. He looked nervous, his eyes never quite connecting with McMasters's eyes, staring instead over his left shoulder.

"You held my room, I hope. I still got two nights paid for."

"Oh, sure, sure. I held it. No skin off my ass if you sleep there or not, long as you pay for it." He retrieved the key from its hook and slapped it on the desk.

McMasters picked it up, hefted it a couple of times, then said, "Good." The kid was staring at the rifle, and McMasters could see that the wheels were turning in his head, but he was afraid to say anything. McMasters walked on to the foot of the stairwell, then started up.

"Will you be needing anything, Mr. McMasters?" the clerk croaked.

"Nothin' but a good night's sleep," McMasters said, moving slowly up the creaking steps. He was tired, and he realized now that the prospect of a bed, an empty one at that, was within reach. He thought about Guadalupe and Margarita, and the little energy left him seemed to evaporate as he reached the top of the stairs.

Walking down the corridor to his room, he shifted the rifle

to his left hand and readied the key in his right. When he reached the door, he stopped, leaned against it for a moment to listen, then unlocked it. Once inside, he dropped his bags on the chair just inside the door, then closed and locked the door and walked to the bed. He set the rifle between the night table and the bed this time, draped his gunbelt over the back of another chair, and started to peel off his clothes.

It was only the middle of the afternoon, but he was exhausted. Pulling off his boots, he set them on the floor beside the bed. Next he stripped off his pants, then lay back, pulling a sheet over his aching bones, leaving the unneeded blanket rolled at the bottom of the bed.

Watching the sun change color through the gauzy curtains for a few moments, he wondered once more if his plan would work. It was complicated, maybe too complicated, but it seemed like the only chance he had. It was cold comfort, but he was too wise to expect anything more.

His eyes closed as the sun changed from orange to red, and before the last red rays stained the curtains for a moment, he was asleep.

He slept fitfully, three times sitting bolt upright, reaching for the rifle before he realized he was alone in his hotel room. Something was gnawing at him, but he didn't know what it was.

He lay there after the third time, listening to the night. The usual scattered sounds of a cow town drifted toward him, almost soothing in their familiarity. He could imagine what it was like in the saloons, how loud the laughter was, how shouted conversations fought with smoke to control the air. But removed like this, all he heard was a subdued mutter, soothing as the surf. Even the jangling piano was too faint to be annoying.

Something tugged at him, made him want to get up and get dressed, go down to the saloon, and bend his elbow a few times. But he knew it was a bad idea. He didn't need to prove to himself any longer that he had won his battle with the bottle. And he didn't need to call attention to himself either. Ben Allison was supposed to keep his whereabouts under his hat, and McMasters was going to lie low until the following day. That was when their plan, such as it was, was to be thrown into gear. Whether those gears would mesh was another matter.

He rolled over onto his stomach, the sheet down around his waist. It was hot, and he was still sweating a little. Despite the open windows, the air in his room was motionless, and still stank of cheap, heavy perfume. It was hard, on these lonely nights, not to think of Hannah. He wondered what his life would have been like if he had never met Rip Winslow. What would the child have been like? Would it have been a boy or a girl? All these questions jostling around the inside of his skull like kernels of corn in a grinder. To look at them from the outside, it was impossible to tell whether they were trying to avoid the rending teeth of the grinder or were eager to be first in line.

That the questions had no answers only made matters worse. They would circle in their bone box forever. If Martha was right, they would grow fainter with time. But it had been almost a year since she'd told him so, and if he paid attention to them, which he tried so hard not to do, they were every bit as deafening as they had been those first few days.

Thank God for Martha, he thought. Somehow, whenever he was on the verge of slipping over the lip of that yawning abyss that he knew lay in wait for him, hoping for one false step, he turned from mourning the dead Hannah to celebrating Martha, so alive in her independence, in the ripeness of her flesh and the richness of her humor. She was what living was all about, and she refused to let him slide off the edge into nothing. He thought about her more when he was away from her like this than when they were together. No amount of lust, however richly rewarded, seemed able to push her out of his mind. As frenzied as his coupling with Guadalupe and Margarita had been, as physically drained as he had been afterward, he still thought about Martha. She was different somehow.

And thinking of the women, he toyed with the notion of going to the cantina again, spending the rest of the night in Guadalupe's bed. He knew that he could lose himself in her for a few hours, even if Margarita weren't there. But it would be a temporary loss, certainly pleasurable but ultimately useless. It would not kill the ache in his heart. Not the one for Hannah, and not the one for Martha.

Walking to the window, he looked out into the night. Leaning out, he saw three saddled horses behind the hotel. It seemed an odd place for them to be. It was nearly midnight, and the horses were just standing free, not hobbled and not hitched. But the reins stretched out oddly toward the wall of the building.

He leaned out still further, but couldn't see what held the reins in place. The horses seemed nervous somehow, as if they were waiting for something, knew something was unusual. One, a big red, pawed the ground, tossing its head and switching its tail energetically. The other two jerked their heads as if trying to free the reins from whatever held them.

McMasters didn't like it. He pulled back inside, and started to dress. He had his jeans on and was stamping down into his boots when he heard something in the hall, not directly outside his room, but not far away either. He buckled on his gunbelt and moved to the door, pressing an ear against it to listen.

He heard whispers, or at least sounds that might have been whispers. The sound was just a sibilant mutter, dampened by the wooden door until it was barely audible. At first, he thought of drunken cowboys stumbling back from a night at the saloon, but drunken cowboys were not so courteous as to whisper. Their conversation would have been raucous enough to wake the dead, or in whispers so exaggerated they would have sounded like shouts. He considered the possibility that someone was trying to coax a woman to his room. That was more likely, but not quite convincing. If a woman had made it to the third floor, she was already convinced.

McMasters waited to hear the grinding of a key in a lock, the click of a latch that would tell him that whoever was in the hall had entered his room. But the corridor was quiet now, even the muttering faded to silence.

Then he thought about the three horses below his window again, knew they were connected to him somehow, and he knew why the reins were reaching toward the rear wall of the hotel—someone was clutching all three sets bunched in his fist, holding the animals quiet while the other two riders went about their business, whatever it was. And now he knew that the muttering in the hall had come from the two men whose horses waited down below his window.

He was starting to back away from the door when he heard the knob rattle. Someone cursed softly. Metal scraped on metal, and a key slid into the lock.

McMasters drew his Colt, holding it high as he pressed his back against the wall three feet from the door frame. He held his breath as the key ground in the lock, its mechanism loose, rattling a little as the key turned. The latch snapped, and someone took in breath with a sharp hiss.

For a long time, McMasters felt as if he had been suspended, as if time had stopped in its tracks. The silence was total now, almost unnaturally so. He considered changing position, but the room was too small and too square to offer him any better cover. At least where he was he had the advantage of surprise.

He brought the gun down, carefully thumbing back the hammer, damping the click with a curved palm. For a moment, he wondered whether he should lie on the floor. Anyone coming through the door would be intent on the bed, assuming him to be sleeping. If McMasters fired from the side, the intruders would turn, probably fire, but well over his head, giving him the chance to get off at least one more shot before they realized where he was.

But he rejected the idea. It was better to be able to move quickly. Three feet from the door, he could hit the intruders from the side and duck out into the hall before they realized he was there. The door started to open now, its hinges creaking a bit. The edge of the door, swollen by the humidity, stuck on the door frame for a moment, then let go, making the door itself shudder as the sudden release caused it to swing open several inches.

Light spilled through the crack, an orange band across the floor, widening as it reached toward the corner of the room. McMasters could see the frayed edge of the faded carpet. Dust motes drifted and swirled in the light. Then shadow blocked the light for a moment. The door swung wider now and a lamp, held high, dangled from a disembodied arm.

McMasters had to struggle against the urge to strike. He wanted to know the odds, assuming there were two men, but not certain. He wanted them inside, where he could see them. The lead man stepped into the room now, raising the lamp still higher as he crossed the threshold.

Behind him, a second man jostled against the first, bumping his companion and making the lamp swing, its handle squeaking twice until the tall man reached out with his gun hand and stopped it.

McMasters glanced toward the bed, trying to see what they saw, and knew that it would not be long before they realized he was not in the bed. Waiting one last instant, just to be certain there were only two, he moved toward the doorway, his boots thumping on the wooden planks.

The shorter intruder heard the sound and turned. It was Carlito. He looked surprised, his mouth open as if he were trying to catch a bug in flight. Then his jaw snapped, and the pistol in his hand swung toward McMasters.

Too late.

McMasters squeezed the trigger, saw the bullet indent the flowery shirt just above the heart, then blood splatter as Carlito began to curl around the point of impact, as if trying to back away from the bullet already shattered inside him and ripping its way through his shoulder blade and splashing gore on the tall man behind him. Carlito's finger jerked convulsively, and his pistol cracked once, the bullet slamming into the wall to the left of the door frame.

The taller man, startled, dropped the lamp, and it shattered on the floor, kerosene spilling in a pool, its sharp tang filling the room. The light guttered, looked as if were about to be extinguished, but the base of the lamp lay on its side, its wick against the edge of the kerosene-soaked carpet.

McMasters was thumbing the hammer for his second shot as the tall man turned, his face suddenly grotesque, lit from below, shadow spilling upward and making his face a mass of orange and black smears, two coal black eyes glittering with reflected light.

One more squeeze of the trigger. Another report as the flames suddenly raced along the edge of the carpet. The tall man opened a black hole in the middle of his face, white teeth glittering for a moment in the bright glare, a soft groan coming from him as he reached for his chest with his free hand. His gun dangled for a moment, caught on his finger by the trigger guard. Then he collapsed to the floor, landing full length and snuffing out six feet of flame as he rolled once and then lay still.

McMasters grabbed the blankets from his bed as footsteps pounded in the hall. He started to beat at the flames, flailing with the rolled cotton, then smothering the kerosene pool and letting it soak into the thick cloth.

He looked up as someone reached the doorway, outlined against the dim light from the lamp in the corridor.

"What the hell's going on, mister? You all right?"

McMasters sighed. "So far," he said.

He went to the window and saw the man far below standing away from the wall now, staring up at him. McMasters leaned out, locking the hammer back, but the man spotted the gun and stepped toward the wall into the shadows. A moment later, footsteps pounded on the sand, receding into the night.

So much for lying low, McMasters thought.

Eighteen

Ben Allison stood off to one side as McMasters explained the rumors he'd been hearing to Miguel Rosales. The foreman looked skeptical, shaking his head from side to side and puffing out his lower lip as if in contempt.

When McMasters finished, Rosales took a deep breath. "So, what you're saying is, you want me to take half a dozen men off the roundup and send them out looking for ghosts, is that it? You want them to keep an eye out for leprechauns too? Maybe there's a pot of gold out there. They see a rainbow, they should come running?"

McMasters held a tight rein on his temper. He'd expected Rosales to be resistant, knowing that it proved nothing. The man had a lot of work to get done, and his reluctance to divert some of his manpower proved nothing. "I just want to make sure we don't get hit by surprise, is all."

"Where did you hear these rumors?"

"Around town."

"Drunken bullshit is what you heard. You ride on over to Morgan Creek and stick your head in the water, you won't have no more trouble like that." He turned then to his boss. "Ben, you think I ought to bother with this garbage?"

Allison shrugged. "I don't know, Mike. What's it hurt? At most, we add another day or so onto the roundup. We're ahead of schedule anyhow. I don't see that it would do no real harm."

"You're the boss." There was an edge to the response, but McMasters didn't want to read anything into it. It could just be exasperation with something Rosales perceived to be stupidity. Turning back to McMasters, Rosales shook his head in resignation. "I'll tell you what, McMasters," he said. "Anything happens, I'll take you to Austin, buy you the best damn dinner you ever ate in your life. But I wouldn't skip meals waiting for that to happen if I was you."

He moved off then, picking half a dozen men at random from the work crew and sending them out in pairs, each to ride one leg of a triangle at the center of which lay most of the Rocking A stock. Rather than come back to join McMasters again, he then turned his attention to reorganizing the work crew around the remaining men.

Allison walked over to McMasters, a thoughtful expression on his face. "That sound like a man who's about to help somebody run off my beeves, Boyd?"

McMasters shook his head. "Can't tell anything from that, Ben, and you know it."

Allison sighed. "Yeah, I know it. I know that. But I still can't believe Mike would be part of something like this. He wouldn't stab me in the back. Not as good as I been to him."

"People will do almost anything for money, Ben. I think you know that too."

Allison ignored the remark. "So what do we do now?"

"Now we wait. I don't expect anything'll happen before dark. If I was going to run off a herd the size my sources were talking about, I sure as hell wouldn't do it in broad daylight."

"Then why in hell disrupt my work crew this morning?"

"Like I said, Ben. I don't know whether Miguel is involved, but I think he might be. And I want him to feel confident. If he thinks he knows what I'm up to, he'll try to work around me, figuring he can outsmart me. That's what I want him to think. Then, if they do strike tonight, we just let them go, follow them until they get to Las Palomas. That's where we make our move."

"I still think it's risky. What if they get my beeves anyhow?"

"Then you're no worse off than you would have been if we hadn't had the warning. And we still have a decent chance to get them back. That's something you wouldn't have had otherwise."

"I wonder if you'd be so damned sure of yourself if they were your cows."

McMasters laughed. "No, I don't think I would, Ben. I guess it's kind of like gambling with house money, isn't it?"

"You got that right," Allison answered. But he laughed in spite of himself. "What you gonna do now?"

"I thought I'd ride back toward San Pedro, see if I spot anything. I imagine they won't come all together. Most likely, they'll ride up by ones and twos, meet someplace, and make their move after dark. We just might get lucky, spot one of them, and follow him to the rendezvous."

"I still think it's risky doing things your way, Boyd."

McMasters nodded. "I know it is, Ben. But it's the only way. You got everything set with the other ranchers?"

"Yep. Soon as we know anything for sure, I'll do like you said and send a runner. Only thing about this botherin' me is, ever'time I look at Mike, I keep wonderin' about how he'd feel if he knew what I was thinkin' and your information is wrong. It'd break his heart. But I guess I got to take the risk."

"One more thing before I go, Ben."

"What's that?"

"You tell anybody I was at the hotel last night?"

Allison looked annoyed. "Hell, no!"

"Nobody at all?"

"You want to speak plain, Boyd, or not? Because if you don't, then I'd just as soon we stop this right here."

"Just answer the question, Ben."

"I mentioned it to Rosalita and Carmen at dinner, is all. Told them you had business in town and that's why you didn't stay with us. Now, do you want to tell me what this is all about or not?"

"I had a couple of visitors last night. They came to my room around midnight. They had a key, which I later found out they got from the clerk after busting him up pretty good. I had to shoot them both. There was a third man with them, but he was downstairs, holding the horses, and he got away."

"You recognize any of 'em?"

McMasters nodded. "One of them was Carlito, the *vaquero* I met on the way out here the first day. I never saw the second man before, and I didn't get a look at the third one clear enough to say."

"Was it that fat man you told me about, Cartwright?"

"No, that much I'm sure of."

"Look, I'm sorry about what happened. But it still don't mean Mike had anything to do with it. I know you're thinkin' maybe Carmen or Rosalita mentioned it to him, but I don't think so. More likely somebody spotted you and sent word. I can ask the gals if you want, but . . ."

"No, don't bother, because I don't want to get him thinking. If we're going to make this work, he's got to think he's got the upper hand."

"If it's him in the first place," Allison reminded him.

McMasters let the remark slide. "I'll be back around sun-down, unless I find something. I'm going to spend a couple of hours out on the open range, and if nothing turns up, I'll go on into town. I'll be at the hotel if you need me before then."

"You be careful, Boyd," Allison warned.

McMasters waved, walked back to the roan, and swung into the saddle. As he rode off, he saw Miguel Rosales watching him, hands on hips. Rosales had not seemed sur-prised to see him, but that proved nothing, because the man who'd escaped might very well have informed him of the failed attack the night before.

Riding in a zigzag pattern, McMasters crisscrossed the ter-rain between San Pedro and the Rocking A. Two hours on the scorched prairie showed him nothing, and he headed for the town. He wasn't tired, but knew he would need his en-ergy later on. He was convinced that if anything was going to happen, it would happen at night, and once it got started, there was no telling when it would all end.

Once in town, he stopped into one of the saloons for a beer, just enough to quench his thirst. While he sat at the bar, he watched the room behind him in the mirror. There were few patrons, and none of them looked out of the or-dinary. There were no familiar faces, but no one gave evi-dence of having ridden a long way either.

Once the beer was gone, he slipped off the stool and walked to the hotel. As he was about to enter the lobby, he saw a lone rider approaching town from the south, and de-cided to sit on the wooden bench until the rider passed. Lean-ing back against the wall, tilting his hat forward, he listened to the buzz of insects in the street, the chirp of a bird he couldn't see, and the noisy swish of tails as the tethered horses tried to keep the flies away.

He could hear the steady clop of hooves approaching, the

rider in no hurry, and after a couple of minutes the rider passed right in front of him. He scrutinized the newcomer from under his hat brim, trying not to be too obvious, and watched as the man passed down the center of the street, dismounted in front of a saloon, and went on inside. He was an Anglo, but McMasters had never seen him before.

After fifteen undisturbed minutes, McMasters went on up to his room and lay down for a nap, leaving his boots on and curling the gunbelt beside him on the bed. The fire had caused no significant damage, but the room smelled of smoke and kerosene. The carpet was gone, and there was a shiny glaze on the floor at the foot of the bed where it had lain.

He closed his eyes, slipping into sleep sooner than he'd expected.

He sat bolt upright a few moments later, or so he thought until he looked at his watch. It was after five, and he cursed himself for being careless. Buckling on his gunbelt, he went down to the lobby and out onto the boardwalk, and looked up and down the street. There were quite a few more horses than there had been earlier, but still nothing out of the ordinary.

McMasters stepped to the roan, booted the big .70-caliber rifle, careful of its telescopic sight, then took a seat on the bench for the second time that afternoon, once more leaning back against the wall behind him and tilting his hat forward against the late afternoon glare.

San Pedro was quiet, but there seemed to be something in the air that McMasters couldn't put his finger on. He couldn't tell whether it was real or a product of his imagination. His expectations could be tricking him into feeling something that wasn't really there. He watched the comings and goings in the street. There was nothing remarkable, no traffic that seemed out of the ordinary, but the feeling persisted.

It was near sundown before he knew that his mind wasn't playing games with him. He heard a few men talking in loud voices some distance down the street. Peering out from under his hat, he recognized Cartwright immediately. Casually, he got up and went into the hotel lobby. Taking a seat on one of the dusty, overstuffed settees haphazardly arranged in the cluttered room, he watched the window for several minutes.

Finally, Cartwright rode past, accompanied by three men, none of whom looked familiar. The fat man looked directly at the window, but the glare of declining sunlight would have made it all but impossible for him to see anyone inside the lobby. When Cartwright rode out of view, McMasters went to the corner of the dusty glass and spotted him a second time, talking to one of his companions, looking for all the world as if he had nothing on his mind but a ride in the evening air.

McMasters waited another minute, then went outside onto the boardwalk. Cartwright was already at the edge of town, and McMasters decided to follow him at a discreet distance. It would be dark soon, and that meant he'd have to stay fairly close. Unhitching the roan, he climbed into the saddle and jerked the reins, wheeling the big stallion about and urging it forward with a squeeze of his knees.

He could just make out four Stetsons and four sets of shoulders as the riders headed down a slight incline, then disappeared below the hilltop. Following in their wake, McMasters walked the roan until he saw the men reappear, moving up the next hill at a slow trot. Once they gained the hilltop, they spurred their mounts and disappeared over the next ridge, in their haste kicking up a little dust now that hung like an orange fog in the slowly fading light.

For the first twenty minutes, McMasters had no trouble keeping them in sight, always a couple of hills away. They did not look behind them, either convinced that their appearance was perfectly innocent, or so confident in their plans they believed they had nothing to fear. Either way, it made McMasters's job a little easier, and he thanked his lucky stars for a small break.

They were halfway between town and the Allison ranch when they changed direction, heading for a stand of cottonwoods on the creek. The light was fading fast now, the few clouds as red-rimmed as weeping eyes, their mass deep purple against the graying sky. The reddish light from the sun, now down on the edge of the world behind him, painted the cottonwood leaves and the peeling bark with a pinkish hue.

As the four men neared the trees, McMasters saw a shadowy figure outlined against the brush, and watched as it moved on foot out into the dying light. There was something familiar about it, but it was too far away from him to be sure. Pulling out the rifle, he dismounted just below a hilltop, crawled to the ridgeline, and lay flat. Picking up the figure in the telescopic sight, he gasped.

It was Mike Rosales. McMasters saw the Rocking A foreman grinning, waving a hand. Cartwright left his three companions and nudged his horse toward Rosales. The foreman stood there talking for a few moments, McMasters trying to read his lips and failing. Rosales nodded when Cartwright said something, then turned and pointed toward the ranch before turning and walking back toward the trees. McMasters lowered the rifle, watching the tableau in miniature now, the figures suddenly shrunken to tiny sticks. Cartwright sat there for a moment, watching Rosales, then raised his hand in some sort of signal.

Before McMasters realized what was happening, the three men opened fire, and he saw Rosales turning, reaching for his gun, then falling to one knee. Cartwright spurred his horse over to the kneeling man and fired point-blank into his face. In an instant it was all over, McMasters staring in disbelief, helpless to prevent it and not daring now to let Cartwright know he had been seen.

Cartwright and his men then spurred their mounts into the brush and crossed the creek as the sun finally slipped away.

Nineteen

McMasters looked behind him at the Allison hacienda. Its lights were fading, and as the big roan crested a hill and started down the other side, they disappeared altogether. Now he was alone in the dark, alone with the look on Ben Allison's face when the big rancher had realized who was draped over the saddle of the horse McMasters was leading. It was a look he didn't think he'd ever forget—pain, anger, confusion, all jumbled together, struggling for dominance, until it looked as if the leathery features of the old Ranger were about to tear themselves apart.

But Allison was tough, tougher than McMasters had expected. He had pulled himself together and sent the runners out, one to gather his own men and the other to pass the word among the rest of the ranchers in the area that it was time to move. McMasters himself was going to ride on ahead, cross the river, and get to Las Palomas for some last-minute reconnaissance. They had a day or two, because it would take that long to push so large a herd all the way to the border and then on to the camp south of Las Palomas, where Don Rosales was scheduled to make payment and take control of the herd.

McMasters knew that it was important that Allison be there to see it for himself, watch with his own eyes as the money changed hands. Only then would any lingering doubts be erased. And only then would Ben Allison accept the harsh reality that his own brothers-in-law had sold him out. That would be the fact. The understanding, if it were to come at all, would come later, but that was Ben Allison's problem, one he would have to wrestle with on his own.

There was some moonlight to guide McMasters, but he still didn't make good time. The barren prairie was almost ghostly under the silvery light. Shapes kept changing. Things that only came out at night darted across the trail, making the roan skittish and winding McMasters himself up tighter than a cheap watch. It was a time to think, especially about things that could not be seen, things that were not at home in the daylight. And McMasters, prone to thinking about such things in the best of times, did not fail to avail himself of the opportunity.

He let the roan set its own pace, knowing that there was no rush, and knowing too that there was very little in his life or his future, however long it might prove to be, that he could control. He understood even less, and began to think of himself as not so much a man with free will as a leaf on a current. He wasn't sure when that change had come about, but knew only that it had been after Hannah's death. Coming to grips with that horror had convinced that he had no say in what happened to him. The logic was simple. If had could control anything at all, her death was the one thing he would have controlled. He would have put his foot down and said no in no uncertain terms.

But he'd had nothing to say about it. Nothing at all. Hannah had been ripped out of his life more surely than the rib had been torn from Adam's side, and with far less reason. With her had gone whatever faith he had possessed, and in that vast emptiness inside him, where his heart had been, a cold stone had been placed—so cold, in fact, that not even Martha Blair could begin to thaw it out.

But in his current job, that cold stone was his one indispensable organ. He needed it to steady him, the way a ship needed ballast to maintain an even keel. He didn't know if it was destined to be there forever, but since he no longer cared much about tomorrow, let alone the day after, it hardly mattered one way or the other. It let him get through the twenty-four hours ahead, that eye-blink beyond which he did not care to look, and it kept him alive, although McMasters wasn't sure that even that mattered very much. As long as he could line up his target in the crosshairs, squeeze the trigger with all the indifference one usually employed in killing a bug or a rat, he would survive.

Looking into the void inside him, he saw, as if he were looking into a brand-new mirror, that he had only one purpose in life, and that was to impose the rule of law from the barrel of a gun. And for such a calling, one did not need a heart. A cold stone would do. He knew he was in a particularly bleak mood, not so much because of what had happened to Miguel Rosales, for that seemed a kind of justice that he could appreciate, but because of what Rosales had showed him about the capacity of a man to betray his own family for a few dollars. In a world where such betrayal was possible, a living, beating heart, after all, was something of a liability, excess baggage at best. Better to live without it.

He was feeling thirsty now, not a thirst for water, but that older, deeper thirst for oblivion that had carried him into the bottle in an attempt to drown himself. One more thing he had been unable to do right. He looked up at the moon, suppressing a shiver. It was nowhere near full, and it looked as if God were winking at him, after a wry joke that only the two of them truly understood. He was tempted for a moment to think that was exactly what it was, until it dawned on him that he no longer believed in God. Such a belief was not rooted in the brain, but in the heart—surely not in a frozen rock.

He pushed the thought aside, trying to concentrate on the plan, trying to visualize it as a way of guaranteeing its success. If he could see it work in his mind's eye, it would work in fact, he told himself.

By the time he reached the Rio Grande, the moon was already sinking on the horizon, its scimitar shape reflected on the water, the smooth blade serrated by the rippling current. He pushed the roan straight ahead into the water, as if he were riding for the moon itself. Holding his rifle overhead, he saw himself on the undulating mirror, like a print from some old history book, some forgotten warrior etched by an anonymous pen, frozen forever in time, locked in immobility so long he no was longer sure who he was or what he was fighting for.

On the far side of the river, he rode on, not worrying about the discomfort of his sopping-wet clothing. He was feeling nothing, his mind concentrating only on the coming confrontation, oblivious to everything but that. He found the Rio San Juan easily, even with the moonlight rapidly declining now, and he was halfway to Las Palomas by the time the moon finally slipped below the hills to the southwest.

The town itself looked better in the dark, better than he remembered it, and as he rode past, he thought for a moment about stopping to see Pedro Morales. But there was no time for such things. He wanted to get to the rustlers' camp and check it out one more time. By morning he wanted to know exactly what he had to do. He wanted to be able to lead the ranchers and their posse to the back end of the valley, sitting behind the camp and its inhabitants like some Damoclean sword poised over their unsuspecting heads.

When he reached the camp, he rode through it, confident that it was deserted, that nothing had changed since the last time he had been there. Dismounting at its center, once more he debated putting it to the torch, and once more rejected the idea, preferring the total surprise on which his plan depended. Even in the dark, the layout came back to him as he walked among the tents and the lean-tos.

He sat there on an upended crate until the black sky began to turn gray, and by the time he had mounted the roan again and nudged it out of camp, the first hint of sunlight had begun to pinken the clouds. He headed back toward Las Palomas, stopping at the dry wash where he had killed the Mexican and dismounting once again to wait for the posse. He saw the cloud of dust that announced their approach a little before eight, and he paced back and forth like an expectant father. Aware of the irony, he kept pushing thoughts of Hannah and his unborn child out of his mind, almost mumbling to himself in his annoyance at their insistent demand for his attention.

Finally, when the posse was little more than a mile away, he remounted and rode north to meet them. Thirty-five men, three of Ben Allison's fellow ranchers among them, armed to the teeth and spoiling for a fight, glared at him suspiciously as he rode up to the point man, a heavyset fellow, Irish by his appearance, and extended his hand.

The Irishman looked at the hand as if it contained a dead fish for a long moment, then fixed his eyes on the visitor. "You McMasters?" he asked, his tone rude enough to suggest he might not believe the answer, whatever it proved to be.

"That's right."

"Ian Flannagan," he said, finally extending his own hand, a freckled slab of ham covered by ginger curls. Flannagan then added, "Lazy F."

Jerking a thumb over his shoulder, Flannagan indicated two other men, who moved forward a little on their mounts. One of them was rail thin, reminding McMasters of a scarecrow. The impression was heightened by a scar on the man's right cheek, running from the corner of his mouth to his right ear. The old wound made it look as if his mouth were only half open when he smiled, as if his cheek could split open all the way to the ear if he were genuinely amused. His yellow hair shot out from under the brim of a Stetson pushed back on his forehead, looking more like straw than anything else. Sticking out a spindly bunch of fingers, he said, "Thomas Haldeman. I own the T Bar H. Pleased to meet you." His accent was German, not unusual in Texas, and McMasters wondered whether the scar was from dueling or from a war wound. It sure as hell wasn't a shaving accident.

The third rancher hung back a bit, just nodding his head to McMasters. His ruddy face looked as if it had been boiled, but the backs of his hands and his forearms, thick as Haldeman's were thin, were bronzed and leathery, "Malcolm Campbell," he announced, in a thick Scottish burr. "C Snake Ranch."

It was clear that both Haldeman and Campbell looked to Flannagan for their lead, and Flannagan was not backward in asserting himself. "All right, suppose you fill us in on what's going on here."

"We should get to the rustlers' camp first."

"Then let's git on with it," Flannagan snapped. "The sooner this is over with, the sooner I can get back to business."

With a nod, McMasters turned the roan around and headed back the way he came, leaving it to Flannagan to marshal his forces and follow in his wake. The aimlessness which had nearly drowned him was gone now, swept away by a wave of energy that seemed to restore his sense of purpose.

He started to push the roan, and only after he'd widened the gap between him and the posse to more than a hundred yards did he think to look around, to make sure they were following him.

Instead of slowing down, he waved his hand overhead, urging the men to close up on him, and angled out into the flats to pass by Las Palomas well to the east. More than likely, someone in the tiny village would spot the cloud of dust, but he'd seen enough of its residents to know that they were none too anxious to poke their noses into a hornets' nest. And it was unlikely that they would say anything to the rustlers, even if some of them stopped in the village on their way to the rendezvous with Don Juan Rosales. It was best, the villagers knew, to see nothing, to hear nothing, and most important of all, to say nothing.

A half mile from the camp, still well to the east to minimize the chance of the rustlers spotting their trail, the posse came to a halt behind McMasters's raised hand. The three ranchers rode up to sit their mounts right beside him, and he handed binoculars to Flannagan, directing him with an extended finger. He waited patiently while Flannagan adjusted the focus and examined the camp. When Flannagan was done, he passed the glasses to Haldeman and then to Campbell.

When all three ranchers had had a look, Flannagan said, "So that's where the weasels live, is it?"

McMasters nodded. "That's it."

"Looks like we can just wait for them to move into camp, then bottle them up. Be like shooting fish in a barrel."

"That's what they count on," McMasters said. "There's a back way out of that canyon. What I think we should do is position ourselves behind the camp, come into the canyon from the southern end, and wait for them to show up. Ben Allison and his men will be behind them, and we'll have them squeezed in a vise. Then, all we have to do is wait for the moneyman to show up. The whole kit and caboodle will be there for the taking.''

''Moneyman, huh? And how the hell are we supposed to know when he's there?''

''I know who he is.''

Flannagan jerked his head around to look sharply at McMasters. ''Who is he?''

''Don Juan Rosales.''

Flannagan's jaw dropped. ''You're shitting me.''

McMasters shook his head. ''I wish I were. But it's true.''

''Allison's brother-in-law?''

''Yep.''

Flannagan shook his head in exasperation. ''I knew it. I knew them damn greaser kinfolk of his were behind it. I kept trying to tell him, but he wouldn't listen.''

''But you didn't have any proof,'' McMasters pointed out. ''You couldn't expect him to turn on his own family without proof.''

''I had all the proof I needed in my gut.''

''That wasn't proof, Flannagan,'' McMasters said. ''It was prejudice.''

''Still and all, it would have saved us a lot of beeves, we'd done what I wanted.''

''That's water under the bridge, Flannagan. Now you have your chance to put an end to the rustling, stop the whole damn operation.''

Flannagan nodded. It was obvious he was unconvinced that waiting had made sense, but the waiting was almost over, and even a stubborn man like Flannagan could see that.

''Let's get moving,'' McMasters said. ''It's a good five or six miles around to the back of the canyon, and I want the dust settled before they show up. They might send a few men on ahead to check things out. And we don't know when

Rosales is gonna show up. And he will probably have a few *federales* with him too. We get into a gunfight, the rustlers will hear it miles away. We'll never get them then.''

"You're in charge, McMasters,'' Flannagan said. "I can't say I like it, but I'll go along . . . for now.''

Twenty

It was a waiting game now, watching the sky for the first telltale signs of the approaching herd. Lookouts had been posted, but everyone was on edge, not knowing what would happen, knowing that almost anything could. McMasters paced back and forth, working off the nervous energy of expectation. He had no way of knowing when the herd would finally cross the river and make its final push toward the camp, and in the back of his mind was the fear that Rosales would bring enough *federales* with him to offset the advantage of surprise.

The *federales* were corrupt—that was undeniable—but they were also trained. Hardly crack troops, they at least had the advantage of a command structure and experience working together under fire. They were not well paid, which would help McMasters, and they were not armed with the most modern weapons. Maybe the edge that counted most, even more than surprise, was that the posse would be fighting for something that belonged to it, anxious to take back what had been stolen, and eager to inflict as much punishment as possible on the men who had done the stealing. Maybe, just maybe, if the pressure was quick enough and relentless enough, the *federales* would be caught up in the chaos and their training would be neutralized. It was a complicated formula, and there was no mathematics that would reveal a single answer in advance.

It was late afternoon when the first lookout spotted the cloud of dust on the horizon. McMasters climbed to the nearest ridge to check it out. Relatively small and coming from the east, it was almost certainly not the herd. Probably Rosales, he thought, as he lifted his binoculars to his eyes and stretched out full length behind some stunted creosote to scan the horizon.

It didn't take him long to pick out the cloud and, once the focus had been adjusted, to spot the small band of horsemen at its bottom. A dozen men at the most, dressed as *vaqueros* but riding with too much precision to be anything other than *federales* out of uniform. Riding at their head, dressed like a prosperous ranchero, was the cause of it all, a man who could not be anyone other than Don Juan Rosales. Even at that range, the resemblance between him and Miguel was remarkable. "Two peas in a pod," McMasters whispered as he adjusted the focus a little, watching the image of the approaching ranchero grow suddenly crystal clear.

Conscious of the scoped .70 beside him, he thought about staying where he was, watching the small band of men draw closer, and when the range was short enough, squeezing the trigger. Chop off the head, after all, and the beast dies. But that would just spook the *federales,* and might prevent recovery of the stolen beeves. McMasters was cold-blooded enough to want it all—Rosales, the herd, and the rustlers— and he'd be damned if he would let his impatience get the better of him.

As he backed away from the ridge and started to get to his feet, he saw Ian Flannagan watching him expectantly. "Well," the big Irishman asked, "what have we got?"

"Rosales and what looks like a dozen *federales* out of uniform."

Flannagan nodded. "So, looks like you're right . . . so far."

"We'll know soon. Pass the word—everybody stays out of sight. I don't want them getting wise before the herd gets here."

"You talk like it's *your* stock been run off."

"Or like a man who takes his job seriously . . . which is exactly what I am."

Flannagan gave him a cold smile, then walked down the hill to spread the word. McMasters stayed on the hillside, watching the excited buzz ripple from man to man a few hundred yards away. Rosales wouldn't enter the camp for another fifteen or twenty minutes, if then. He might decide to swing north and meet the herd, ride the last few miles along with his latest catch.

But the cloud kept on heading toward the mouth of the canyon, and McMasters soon decided Rosales was going to wait at the camp. Now, the only hitch was the possibility that Cartwright had spotted Ben Allison and the second half of the posse riding behind the herd, McMasters crossed his fingers, looked at the sky for a moment, then reached for a Primero. He lit it, took a few quick puffs, then stubbed it out, too anxious to draw any comfort from the harsh tobacco.

Walking along the ridgeline, McMasters took up a position that allowed him to look down into the camp. He found some cover in a niche among several large boulders, and waited for Rosales to arrive. He didn't have to wait long.

The ranchero rode in at the head of his dozen men, and his easy familiarity with the layout showed just how acquainted he was with the place. The small band dismounted, and started to remove the tack from their horses. Obviously, Rosales planned to stay the night. This was a break,

McMasters thought. Unhorsed, the *federales* would be at a disadvantage when push came to shove.

The men disappeared into the tents and lean-tos, Rosales himself entering the largest tent alone. Fifteen minutes later, the first smudges of the advancing herd stained the northern horizon. From the rapidly increasing size of the dust cloud, it was apparent that the herd was a large one, and moving at a good clip.

McMasters decided that the last piece of puzzle had just fallen into place. If the rustlers had learned of Allison's pursuit, they would have lost time in fighting off the old Ranger and his men, but they were ahead of schedule. So far, so good, McMasters thought. Now, all he had to do was bide his time.

He saw one of the lookouts scrambling down the steep side of the canyon, passing the word to Flannagan and the others, now concealed on both sides of the rear exit, waiting as impatiently as McMasters himself.

The herd was coming on hard, the dust thickening like a gathering storm. Soon, McMasters knew, he would hear the muted bellowing of the beeves, the piercing whistles and strident yips of the drovers. Backing out of the niche, he crouched low and walked along the ridge, dodging in and out among the boulders, using the stunted creosote and scrub brush for cover, and when he was far enough away from the camp to minimize the risk of being seen, he skidded downhill.

Flannagan came to meet him. "Where the hell you going in such a hurry?" he asked.

"I'm going out the back way, circle the herd, and hook up with Ben. Once he knows you and your men are in place, we can make our move. As long as you're patient, I don't see how we can miss."

"You be careful, McMasters. And tell Ben nobody blames

him for this. Not no more. Seems like maybe he was used worse than any of us.''

McMasters nodded. "Keep your head down, Mr. Flanna-gan."

The big Irishman grinned. "Hard enough, takes more than a bullet to bust this old skull," he said.

McMasters unhitched the roan and swung into the saddle. It would take him nearly a half hour to work his way around. Then, once he got past the herd, he had to find Allison. The plan was to meet him at the dry wash, and he hoped like hell that Allison would be there.

He used the dust kicked up by the herd as the focus of his circle, heading northeast until the cloud was due west, then angling back in behind it. He could hear the beeves clearly, even the thunder of their hooves. The shrill whistles of the drovers now seemed to goad him as much as they did the cattle.

Behind the herd now, far enough away that he couldn't be seen, he headed directly for the wash. How long he would have to wait depended on just how far behind Allison was. Knowing Ben, it wouldn't be too long a wait. Rangers, re-tired or otherwise, were not known for their patience, and Ben Allison, as one of the best, was likely one of the least patient. He would almost certainly have stayed as close as he could, even close enough to see the drag rider.

McMasters struck the wash a good half mile from the Rio San Juan, and followed its southern lip. He reached the man-made passage, and realized he was now well west of the herd. It hadn't dawned on him that driving the beeves across the wash would have been risky, and that Cartwright must have had another route that enabled him to bypass it. But even as McMasters watched, he could tell that the herd had now angled west, straight toward the canyon camp.

Impatient himself, McMasters paced back and forth in the

bottom of the wash. He thought about heading north, trying to pick Ben up sooner, but if he missed the connection, it would only slow things further. He walked ten yards in one direction, and twenty back, then turned and retraced his steps. Each time he reached the midpoint, he walked partway up the slope to see over the lip of the wash. On his fifth climb, he saw Ben Allison well out ahead of his men. When Allison spotted him, he turned and waved his hat, urging his men to hurry.

McMasters climbed out of the wash and stood waiting. Allison reined in, dismounted, and reached out a hand. "How's it look, Boyd?" he asked.

"Flannagan and the others are all set. All we have to do is let Cartwright drive the herd into the canyon, and we can stick the cork in, bottle them up."

Allison looked thoughtful. "I still don't mind telling you I have a hard time believing that Juan Rosales is behind all this."

"I saw him with my own eyes not an hour ago, Ben."

Allison nodded sadly. "I know it's true. I just . . . awww, hell, never mind!"

"How do you want to handle it from here on?"

"I want to ride right into this here camp and look Juan in the eye, tell him what a damned skunk I think he is, then shoot the sonofabitch."

"We can't shoot them all."

"Why the hell not?"

"You know the answer to that as well as I do."

"Yeah, I do, I know I do, but that don't mean I have to like it."

"If we get Rosales and Cartwright, that'll put an end to it. Rosales is the mastermind and the moneyman. Cartwright is his right-hand man. The rest of them are just cowboys.

With the leaders gone, the rustling is done. We'll break their back.''

"Look, I suppose there's some sort of jurisdiction bullshit here, but . . ."

"Not for me. I'm authorized to do whatever I have to. I bring Rosales and Cartwright back for trial, they'll stand trial. You can bank on that."

"I know Juan. He's a hard man. I don't think you'll be taking him back, unless it's in a goddamned box. And that is fine by me."

"You ready?"

"Ready as I'll ever be."

"Then let's get moving," McMasters said. He walked back into the wash, climbed into the saddle, and nudged the stallion up the far side, then waited for Allison and his men to negotiate the steeply canted passage, counting them by twos as they crossed.

Once all the men were across, McMasters turned toward the camp. Allison was beside him, and leaned over. "Let's just ride full tilt into the middle of the damn camp, put the fear of God into them."

"It's your decision, Ben."

"Fine, then that's my decision."

The closer they came, the harder the men pushed their horses. The dust from the huge herd had already begun to settle, but some of it drifted on the hot breeze, getting in their eyes and coating their sweating skins with brownish paste. When the mouth of the canyon came into view, McMasters pointed, shouting, "There it is!"

Allison nodded, then spurred his mount into a full gallop, raising his hand overhead, then stabbing it forward as the charge began. Entering the canyon, McMasters saw the stunned looks on the faces of the rustlers, most of whom were still unsaddling their mounts. He saw the fat man, Cartwright, standing at the entrance to the large tent Juan Rosales had gone into earlier.

Cartwright shouted something into the tent, then began to scurry around among his men, who grabbed for their weapons. Ben Allison opened fire, heading straight down the middle of the camp, wheeling his mount at the far side, then charging back. Sporadic fire opened up from the disorganized rustlers, but it was no match for the furious volleys from the charging posse.

Juan Rosales rushed out of his tent and shouted for his men to form up. The *federales* responded, forming a double line. Rosales moved to one side and gave a command, and the front rank dropped to one knee.

Their old weapons snapped into line and at a command, the front rank fired. One of Allison's men was knocked from his horse, and McMasters saw the wounded man scramble in behind a battered lean-to, bleeding from the shoulder.

McMasters opened up on the *federales,* taking three down with three quick shots. The tight formation broke then, the men turning their backs and running in among the tents. Allison rallied his men into a tight cordon across the mouth of the canyon, herding the rustlers back in among the tents and then beyond. Some were already running for the exit. McMasters hoped that Flannagan was ready, and when half a dozen men sprinted around the canyon wall and disappeared, a furious volley erupted. Four of the fleeing men stumbled back the way they'd come. Others rushed past them, only to be driven back by the relentless fire from the steep walls of the canyon. They had no cover, and no one to tell them what to do.

Already, hands were starting to be raised as several of the rustlers threw down their weapons. Juan Rosales was furious. He stalked back and forth among the tents, trying to gather his men for a counter-thrust, but they were having none of it. He saw Allison, smiled, and stood his ground as the old Ranger rode right up to him, keeping his pistol steady, the muzzle aimed at Rosales's midsection.

Twenty-one

"You bastard," Allison hissed. "How the hell could you do this to me?"

"Do what?" Rosales challenged. "What did I do? You took our land and thought it was yours. Now am I planning to take it back."

"That was never your land, Juan."

"*Sí,* it was Mexico, until you *Tejanos* came and stole it. You stole from us, and so I stole from you."

Allison dismounted, never taking his gaze off Rosales. McMasters stood to one side, watching the tortured expression on Allison's face, the arrogant disdain, mixed with contempt, that twisted Rosales's face into a sneer.

The shooting had stopped now. McMasters saw that the posse had herded the rustlers all together. Holding them at gunpoint, several of the members of the posse were moving among the forest of upraised arms, gathering the weapons tossed to the ground, lugging them to the middle of the camp, where they made a heap in front of the main tent.

"Family, Juan, I'm your *family*!" Allison said, his voice betraying his inability to understand. "For Christ's sake!"

"You are no family of mine, Allison. You sleep with my

sister. That is all. And that is her fault, not mine.''

''But Miguel, he worked with me. For almost twenty
years. I treated him like a son!''

At the mention of Miguel, Allison shook his head, and
Rosales seemed to sense that there was something he didn't
know. He wanted to ask Allison what was wrong, why he
had reacted that way, but seemed unable to speak for a moment. When he did, it was to spew more vitriol.

''You treated him like a mule. What do you think it was
like for him, to take orders from you, to accept a wage as
if he were no more than some drunken *vaquero*? He was a
proud man, a Rosales, and you rubbed his nose in the
dirt.''

McMasters moved into the crowd of rustlers then, looking
for Cartwright. He found the fat man in the middle, doing
his best to seem inconspicuous. McMasters grabbed him by
the arm and started to drag him out of the crowd. Cartwright
attempted to resist, but McMasters prodded him in the gut
with the barrel of his Colt, and the fat man finally caved in,
stumbling out into the clear, then toward Rosales and Allison, propelled by several more pokes of the pistol.

Both Allison and Rosales turned to watch the stumbling
fat man approach, McMasters behind him, driving him re-
lentlessly forward with jabs of the pistol barrel into the small
of his back.

Allison broke the silence. ''Boyd, what the hell are you
doing?''

Looking at Rosales instead of Allison, McMasters answered. ''I thought the Don might want to meet the man
who killed his brother. He seems to think Miguel deserved
more than you gave him. Maybe it was the bullet in the
head from Cartwright here. Maybe that's what he deserved.''

Rosales looked stunned then. His lips trembled, his jaw

seemed to quiver as if something were trying to shake it loose from his skull.

"Miguel dead? Is this true?" Rosales didn't know where to look. He stared at Cartwright for a long moment, then looked to McMasters, who canted his head toward the old Ranger as if to say, "There's the man who will tell you."

Ben Allison nodded slowly. "It's true, Juan. Miguel is dead."

"But . . . when . . . how? This can't be!"

"I'm afraid it is, Juan. McMasters here saw it happen. Your man Cartwright met him a couple of miles from my ranch last night—to arrange this raid, I figure—and then, when they were done talkin', some of Cartwright's boys opened fire on him."

"But you said it was Cartwright who killed him." Rosales was staring intently at the fat man now, trying to look inside him, and at the mention of his name, Cartwright flinched, involuntarily raising his arms as if to ward off a blow.

It was McMasters who responded. "That's right. When Miguel was down, Cartwright rode right up to him and fired point-blank. He never had a chance."

Rosales moved then, hurling himself at the fat man, who once more raised his arms. As if unaware of the pistol still clenched in his fist, Rosales grabbed Cartwright by the throat and began to squeeze. "You bastard!" Rosales screamed. "Why? You bastard, you fat gringo pig! Why?"

Cartwright had his hands locked around Rosales's wrists, his head tilted to avoid the pistol's hammer digging into his throat. In a choking voice, he grunted, "You said it was finished. You said to wrap it up. I thought . . ."

But Rosales wanted to hear no more. He squeezed still harder, and Cartwright broke off in a strangling gurgle.

Allison moved in to break it up, but Rosales turned on

him, fired once at the rancher, then shot Cartwright twice in the face, the second bullet smashing through the bridge of the fat man's nose and splattering gore in every direction.

Allison clutched his arm and went down to one knee. McMasters raced toward him. "Ben, Ben, are you all right?"

The canyon was suddenly silent, the echo of Rosales's pistol shots fading away like clapping hands far in the distance, then dying altogether. Allison tried to get back to his feet, and suddenly raised his pistol, but McMasters was crouched over him, and he couldn't get a clear shot.

"Get him, Boyd," Allison whispered. "The sonofabitch is getting away."

McMasters turned to see Rosales running through the milling crowd of rustlers, who seemed uncertain whether to join their leader in his flight or to count their lucky stars and stay put.

McMasters raced after him, firing one shot in the air. "Rosales," he shouted, "stop!"

Rosales turned and fired wildly over his shoulder, hitting one of his own men in the back, then dodging to one side before McMasters could return fire.

As he raced through the crowd, McMasters kept his pistol ready, his eyes on the place where Rosales had last been, and didn't notice one of the rustlers extend a foot. Tripping over the outstretched heavy boot, McMasters sprawled in the dirt, losing his grip on the Colt. He scrambled after the pistol on all fours, got to his feet again, and shoved roughly through the closing crowd.

Waving the pistol menacingly, he charged on, the prisoners parting reluctantly but surely as the ugly black eye of the Colt's muzzle stared at each man for an instant before moving on.

Breaking through the rear of the crowd, he saw Rosales

already heading around the bend in the canyon, and he ran faster, trying to close the gap before the Mexican could find cover and ambush him.

He skidded to a momentary halt just before the bend in the wall, heard the crunch of fleeing footsteps, and realized that Rosales was more intent on escape than bushwhacking him. He sprinted around the corner. Once more, he raised his pistol into the air and fired a warning shot. Rosales looked back once, his face contorted by the effort of running. It was obvious that he was tiring, and the Mexican sprinted another fifty yards before turning to face him, pistol in hand. He was panting, and in the reddish light of early evening, beads of sweat glistened on his skin like tiny rubies.

"Give it up, Rosales!" McMasters shouted. He sprinted ahead, closing to within fifty feet of the breathless don.

Rosales laughed. "I don't think so, gringo." He took a step forward, then ducked to the left as McMasters snapped off a shot.

Grinning now, Rosales started toward him, waving his pistol as if it were a magic wand and he expected McMasters to disappear. "You have overplayed your hand, gringo," he said.

Rosales walked quickly now, until he was no more than ten feet away. Smiling almost pleasantly now, he thumbed back the hammer on his pistol. It was very casual, even off-handed. "You see, gringo, I can count. You are out of bullets because you gringos are all the same. You think that you are invincible. And now you will have to pay the price for your arrogance."

"You sure about that, Rosales?" McMasters asked, thumbing back the hammer on his own gun.

"As I said, gringo, I can count. You are so sure of yourself, you think some poor *Mexicano* does not know how to count to six. Good-bye, gringo . . .''

And McMasters squeezed the trigger. The seventh round in his rechambered cylinder hammered home, ripping into the stunned don's chest, exploding his breath out in a surprised ''Oooohhh!'' Then he fell to the ground, his eyes wide open, already sightless as McMasters stood over him and holstered his Colt.

''Things are not always as they seem, Don Rosales,'' he whispered.

Turning then, McMasters walked slowly back toward the camp. As he rounded the bend, he saw Ian Flannagan running toward him, followed by a couple of cowboys.

''You all right, McMasters?'' he shouted.

McMasters nodded. ''Fine.''

''You get him?''

''Yep. How's Ben?''

''He'll be all right. Bullet missed bone, just tore up the meat in his shoulder. He's already cussing and fussing.''

''I guess it's over then.''

''I reckon. We found a bunch of money in Rosales's saddlebags. Not enough to pay for all the stolen beeves, but damn close. And we got this herd back, so I reckon things'll work out just about even. Ben figures, as long as we come this far, we might as well push the herd on into Matamoros.''

McMasters moved on past him, walked back to the camp, and found Ben Allison sitting on a sour-smelling bunk in one of the tents. ''How you feeling, Ben?'' he asked.

''About like I been shot at and hit.'' He laughed. ''How about you?''

''I'm fine.''

''We're gonna go on downriver to the coast with the herd. You comin'?''

McMasters shook his head. "Nope. I got a couple of people to see."

"What, here?"

"I made a promise to a friend in Las Palomas. Figure I'll stop buy and let him know I kept it. Then I think I'll be heading home."

Twenty-two

He rode all night, something pulling him forward, something he understood, although he did not know how to name it. It was near dawn before he found a place to camp, planning to stay just long enough to get a bit of sleep and rest the roan.

When he woke up, it was just about noon. As he stood beside the ashes of his campfire, he cast almost no shadow at all, just a dark smudge a couple of inches wide. It was as if the sun had hammered him flat, or driven him like a spike into the rocky ground.

He drank some cold coffee, then saddled the roan, not caring that it was going to be boiling hot out on the plains. There was someplace he wanted to be, and he would do whatever he had to do to get there. The sooner the better.

He thought about Ben Allison, wondered how the old man was going to tell his wife that both her brothers were now gone, his daughter that she had no uncles now. Then, as much as he felt for the old Ranger, he pushed the thoughts aside. Pedro Morales had his sorrow and, God knows, McMasters had his own. But right now, there was no room in his life for sorrow.

Instinctively, he clutched his chest, as if feeling for that cold stone among his ribs, and realized that it was neither as hard nor as frozen as he sometimes thought. It was Martha, of course, that lured him on, not just the woman, not just the honey hair and the ample flesh, the full, perfect breasts, and the damp moss between her thighs. It was not just his desire for her body. It was the laugh, the sparkle in her eye, the soft down on her muscular arms that shone like gold in the sunlight and was turned silver by the moon. It was everything about her—in short, it was the idea of her.

He felt something for her that he could not put into words, and there was only one word he knew that came close to summing it up, a word that he still shied away from. He sometimes thought that to give voice to his feelings would somehow doom them, as if he were somehow unworthy of Martha Blair and to acknowledge how he felt would be the one arrogant act that would prove it, and place her forever beyond his reach.

It was near nightfall by the time he saw the small house, the orange light in the window making the gauzy curtains look as if they had been spun from the finest gold. Once, still half a mile away, he thought he saw her shadow on the curtains, and something jumped in his chest, but he resisted the urge to push the exhausted horse any faster.

Not until he rode up to the tiny house and began to dismount did the door open. He looked up and saw her, arms flecked with white froth, dusted with flour.

"Baking something, are you?" he said.

"What if I am?" She laughed. "Don't go thinking it's for you."

"It isn't?"

"Not necessarily."

He unsaddled the roan and hung the tack on a wooden rack under the canted eaves. "And why not?"

"Who ever knows when you'll come back?"

"I notice you didn't say home," he teased.

"This is your home, is it? I don't think so. You're not here often enough."

He stepped onto the porch, wrapped her in his arms, and lifted her off her feet.

"You'll get flour all over you," she said, giggling, wiping one wrist on his forehead, leaving the sweet smell of sugar behind.

"I've gotten worse things on me, Martha."

"Then I guess it'll be all right."

He set her down, tugged at her apron strings, and peeled the apron away.

"You're awfully familiar this evening, Mr. McMasters."

"Not as familiar as I'll be in the morning."

"And sure of yourself, too."

But she reached for the first button on her bodice as he slipped past her and into the house.